"I think I should go toward the house. I need you to trust me on this, Wyatt," Abby whispered.

Fear lodged in his throat. He snagged her arm. "Please stick with me."

"I won't be long." She shook off his hand and darted forward.

He pulled his weapon and prepared to follow. Running silently, he held his breath until he reached the house, too.

Peering around the corner, he expected to see Abby, but there was no one there. He inched forward when he saw movement in the trees. He instinctively dropped to the ground, just as a crack of gunfire rang out.

He sprang up and threw his leg over the sill of an open window. Ducking beneath the glass, he fell into the room as a second crack of gunfire rang out.

"Wyatt?" Abby called softly.

"Stay down." Another gunshot came from what sounded like the front of the house.

If they didn't find a way to escape, they'd be trapped!

Laura Scott has always loved romance and read faith-based books by Grace Livingston Hill in her teenage years. She's thrilled to have been given the opportunity to retire from thirty-eight years of nursing to become a full-time author. Laura has published over thirty books for Love Inspired Suspense. She has two adult children and lives in Milwaukee, Wisconsin, with her husband of thirty-five years. Please visit Laura at laurascottbooks.com, as she loves to hear from her readers.

Books by Laura Scott

Love Inspired Suspense

Hiding in Plain Sight
Amish Holiday Vendetta
Deadly Amish Abduction
Tracked Through the Woods

Justice Seekers

Soldier's Christmas Secrets
Guarded by the Soldier
Wyoming Mountain Escape
Hiding His Holiday Witness
Rocky Mountain Standoff
Fugitive Hunt

Pacific Northwest K-9 Unit

Shielding the Baby

Visit the Author Profile page at LoveInspired.com for more titles.

TRACKED THROUGH THE WOODS

LAURA SCOTT

LOVE INSPIRED SUSPENSE

INSPIRATIONAL ROMANCE

LOVE INSPIRED® SUSPENSE
INSPIRATIONAL ROMANCE

Recycling programs for this product may not exist in your area.

ISBN-13: 978-1-335-59907-0

Tracked Through the Woods

Love Inspired
22 Adelaide St. West, 41st Floor
Toronto, Ontario M5H 4E3, Canada
www.LoveInspired.com

Printed in U.S.A.

We will rejoice in thy salvation,
and in the name of our God we will set up our banners:
the Lord fulfil all thy petitions.
—*Psalm* 20:5

This book is dedicated to Marcia Johnson in Fort Wayne, Indiana. Thanks for being such a special friend to Vicki and Sally! Any friend of theirs is a friend of mine.

ONE

Abby Miller stealthily approached the log cabin in the north Wisconsin woods. She'd been searching for her father, Peter Miller, since her last phone conversation with him had abruptly cut off, as if someone had grabbed the phone from his hand. Then, when she'd tried to call him back there had been no answer.

As the days stretched into weeks, an overwhelming sense of dread had washed over her. It wasn't like her dad to completely sever all ties with her. Not for this length of time.

Every instinct in her body screamed that something had gone terribly wrong.

After several failed attempts to find him, Abby had decided to backtrack to every place they'd ever used as a temporary safe house during those years they'd hidden from the Chicago mafia.

Which had brought her here, to this remote cabin nestled in the woods. The scent of wood burning, combined with the thin trail of smoke from the chimney, indicated the cabin was not empty.

Someone was inside.

Her father? Or someone else?

For years, she and her father had been on the run from the Marchese organized crime family. Her dad was a Marchese himself, but escaped from the mob life at eighteen. He'd hidden out in an Amish community, becoming so enmeshed in the plain life that he'd married and had twin daughters, Abby and her sister Rachel.

He would have stayed there, too, if the Marchese family hadn't found him. But they had. Forcing him to leave with Abby, raising her alone.

This past year he'd gone to the FBI to provide key information to take the Marchese family down once and for all. His first meeting with Agent Wyatt Kane had gone well. The second, not so much. When gunfire rang out with Kane nowhere nearby, her father knew he'd been betrayed by Agent Wyatt Kane.

She and her father had split up for safety reasons, but had kept in touch. Until now.

Deep down, she couldn't ignore the possibility her father had been killed. The thought of a dirty FBI agent attempting to kill her dad made her angry.

Yet she tried to remain positive. Her father was smart, and an expert at staying off grid. She needed to have faith in his ability to escape.

Darkness had fallen well over an hour ago, the low full harvest moon glowing bright in the velvet sky. She stepped cautiously across the soft pine needles and fallen leaves blanketing the earth. Using the trees for cover until reaching the clearing, she crouched and debated which window to approach first.

Envisioning the interior where they'd stayed several months when she was young helped her to identify that the window located directly ahead belonged to one of the two bedrooms. She had no idea which one the occupant was using, but it was a good starting point. Just as she rose to creep forward, a twig snapped behind her.

Dropping to the ground, she made herself as small as possible behind the tree. The tiny hairs on the back of her neck lifted in alarm. It wasn't as if the woods were quiet—foxes, coyotes and white-tailed deer roamed freely here. There were no doubt black bears and bobcats, too.

Yet she sensed a human had made the noise, not an animal.

The seconds dragged by as she remained curled in a ball behind the tree, every one of her senses on alert. She'd left her vehicle a solid two miles away and hadn't noticed anyone following her from the Twin Cities.

Maybe the cabin resident was out and about, checking the perimeter. It's what she'd have done if she were staying there. And it was something her father would have done, too. It gave her hope that maybe he was safe after all.

Still, she didn't move, waiting and watching for the person inside to show himself.

A full fifteen minutes passed. Belching tree frogs and the occasional hoot of an owl echoed around her, but no sign of a person.

Abby let another long stretch of time pass before slowly rising from the ground. Maybe the twig had been broken by a wild animal. One thing for sure, an innocent person returning home would have continued moving toward the cabin, rather than hiding out.

The thought was not reassuring.

Swallowing the urge to call out to her dad, she drew in a deep breath, rose and quickly crossed the clearing, pressing herself up alongside the cabin. Again, she waited, to see if anyone else followed her.

Nothing moved. So far, so good.

Sliding along the cabin wall, she turned slightly to peer through the window. It wasn't easy to see in the darkness, but after a long moment, she confirmed the room was empty.

Flattening herself back against the wall, she quickly passed the window to check the next one. That room was empty, too.

Her pulse kicked up with anticipation. Maybe her dad was here! He could have gone out to check the perimeter just as she'd approached.

Although if that was the case, why hadn't he answered any of her phone calls?

After another long five minutes, she eased around the corner of the cabin to approach the back door. Getting inside would be the best way to prove her father was staying there.

Testing the doorknob, she frowned. It wasn't locked. That gave her pause, but then she pushed the door open and peeked inside.

The scent of burning wood was stronger now, a faint glow coming from the cast iron stove in the corner. She slipped inside and closed the door, taking a moment to search for personal items.

The interior was clear. Not a single item of clothing, a book, or slip of paper indicated anyone was living there. If not for the stove being full of wood and lit for warmth, she'd have assumed the place to be vacant.

Crossing the main room housing the small kitchen and living space, she checked both bedrooms. The covers on the bed in the first room were dusty and had obviously not been recently disturbed.

The second room, though, was different. While the bed was made, the bedding looked and smelled clean rather than musty. Yet there were no items of clothing in this space, either.

What in the world?

With a deep frown, she left the bedroom to return to the main living quarters.

"Hello, Abby."

She stopped dead, her gaze fixated on the tall stranger standing in the center of the room. Her blood ran cold as she realized her situation had gone from bad to worse.

"You must be FBI Agent Wyatt Kane." She forced the words through her tight throat. It wasn't a stretch, based on the gun clipped to his belt and the way his dark hair was neatly trimmed. All that was missing was the obligatory blue suit. He was dressed in jeans, a flannel shirt and dark jacket but she still figured he was a fed.

His eyes widened in surprise, but he nodded. "You're good, Abby, I'll grant you that. I am Special Agent Kane."

She tried not to stare at his gun, desperately wishing for a weapon of her own. Why wasn't he using it to threaten her? She had no doubt he intended to silence her and her father, once and for all.

Well, if that was the case, she wasn't going down without a fight. She lifted her chin and met his gaze defiantly. "What are you waiting for?"

He frowned. "What are you talking about? I'm here to find your father, same as you."

She was glad her dad wasn't in the cabin, if he'd even been there at all. "You'll never find him. How could you set him up to be killed? Are you working for the Marchese crime family? Did you do all of this for money?"

"I didn't set your father up, Abby. I didn't try to shoot him. I know that's what he thinks, but it wasn't me." Wyatt Kane lifted his hands palm out. "I have reason to believe the leak within the agency is my boss, Ethan Hawthorne. And I was hoping your father could help me prove it."

His comment knocked her off balance, although she tried hard not to show it. Was this some sort of trick? She didn't trust Wyatt as far as she could throw him.

Yet his identifying his boss as the real culprit was an interesting twist.

Either way, she wasn't about to lower her guard. Quite the opposite. She shifted her feet so that she could spring into action if needed. "Yeah, well, as you can see, my father isn't here."

"But you thought he might be."

She was irritated this dirty FBI agent had managed to find the cabin. She had to give him credit—she honestly had not anticipated this.

"Now what?" She changed the trajectory of the conversation. "Are you going to arrest me? Or just shoot me?"

"As far as I know, you haven't broken the law, so there's no reason to arrest you. And of course I'm not going to shoot you. I'm not the bad guy here, Abby. Ethan Hawthorne is."

"If you say so." Was this some story he was spinning so he could get close to her father? Eliminating her wouldn't help keep his secret safe, unless he silenced her father, too.

No way was she falling for his act.

With Wyatt Kane standing in front of the back doorway, escaping that way wasn't an option. And the front door was also a poor choice as he was closer to it than she was. Maybe through one of the bedroom windows, as they were located behind her, but it was doubtful she'd have the time to wrench one open and climb out before he caught her.

Unless she could come up with a diversion.

He took a step toward her. She instinctively moved back, but also a few inches to the right side to get closer to the wood-burning stove. There were several split logs stacked on a pile there, about the only item remotely close enough to be used as a weapon.

"Who else knew about your meeting with my father that day?" She moved another inch as she tried to distract him with questions. "You claimed my dad would be safe speaking with you. Yet as he approached your meeting spot, shots rang out, narrowly missing him."

"I know. That was unfortunate."

"Unfortunate?" She scoffed, taking another step backward. "That's an understatement."

"Abby, please. I'm telling you the truth." His gaze implored her to believe him. "I want to bring Ethan Hawthorne down as much as your father does. As much as you do. But I need help. I need proof."

"Shouldn't the FBI be able to help with that?" She eased another inch to the right. "Don't they have some sort of internal affairs department like the police do? My father can't help you, and neither can I."

"I can't go to anyone within the Bureau, as I have no idea who else might be involved." He took another step, and that was all the impetus she needed.

She lunged to the right, grabbed a log and tossed it toward him. Her goal wasn't to hurt him, but to distract him. Without hesitation she made a run for the closest bedroom. She yanked hard on the window, and it lifted with a groan of protest. Throwing her leg over the sill, she ducked, then brought the other leg through the opening.

"Abby! Wait!"

Ignoring Agent Kane's shout, she bolted for the woods, as if a hungry pack of wolves nipped at her heels.

Wyatt lunged for the window, but he was too late. With amazing athleticism, Abby Miller had gotten through. He refused to give up, though, crawling through the window with far less nimbleness to follow her.

He needed Abby and her father. He couldn't fight Hawthorne alone. All he had was suspicion, especially after the way Hawthorne had turned on him, dragging Wyatt's name through the mud. As if his boss was deflecting his own criminal activity to Wyatt. There was nothing worse than a dirty cop and he would not rest until he had the evidence he needed to bring Hawthorne down.

Unfortunately, Abby was a worthy foe. As was her father. Not that he wanted to be at odds with either of them. If he could just get her to listen to reason. They were all on the same side. Hawthorne must be stopped, before anyone else was hurt.

Abby disappeared into the woods. He followed, listening intently to the sounds of her footsteps.

But then they halted. Or she was stepping so quietly he could no longer hear her.

This was not how this was supposed to go, he thought grimly. She didn't understand that Hawthorne had nothing to lose and everything to gain by eliminating her and her father.

Maybe Wyatt, too, if his boss believed he was on to him.

Slowing his pace, he scanned the woods, searching for a clue as to where Abby had gone. He felt certain she'd eventually make a break for her vehicle, so he turned and cut through the woods in a direct path toward her car, determined to meet up with her there.

He should have anticipated she'd attempt to escape. Throwing the log in his direction had forced him to rear back and deflect it, giving her just the head start she'd needed.

As angry as he was with having to chase Abby down, he couldn't help but admire her. Somehow, he needed to make her understand he wasn't the bad guy. He'd thought that not using his weapon would reassure her.

Apparently not.

He put on a burst of speed, doing his best to move quickly and silently. He needed to reach her vehicle as soon as possible. If Abby escaped the area, he'd find her car as he had the license plate number, but if she ditched the sedan for something else, he'd end up back at square one.

A tiny voice in the back of his mind warned him she may just give up the car now, rather than using the rusty sedan as an escape route. But they were easily ten miles or more from civilization and the unincorporated town of Pilgrim was barely a dot on a map.

At the same time, he doubted staying in the woods all night would bother her. Abby was a tough cookie. Based on the merry chase she'd led him over several state lines, he wouldn't put anything past her.

Stumbling over a fallen log, he twisted his ankle, yet managed to stay upright. Ahead, moonlight filtered through the trees. He pushed forward, ignoring the pain in his left leg. There was a twenty-foot clearing between the woods and the side of the road. He was almost there.

At the edge of the woods, he paused, then smiled in satisfaction when he noticed Abby's rusty sedan was still there.

Slowing his pace and favoring his left ankle, he kept moving while scanning the area. There was no sign of Abby, at least not yet. His SUV was parked a half mile down the road and around a curve, well out of sight.

He made his way to the sedan, then hunkered down behind it, using the rear tire and the sedan itself to hide from view. While he'd moved as silently as possible, she might assume he'd end up here at her vehicle. Regardless, he'd rather wait out of sight, hoping he could convince her to listen to reason.

For the second time that night, the minutes passed with painstaking slowness. His earlier patience had at last been rewarded when Abby had finally darted toward the cabin. But as the seconds ticked by, he wondered if that had been a one-time thing.

Abby could be hiding in the woods right now, determined to stay there indefinitely.

His left ankle throbbed, forcing him to kneel on the asphalt road.

After ten minutes he began to doubt the

wisdom of his plan. Peering over the top of the sedan, he swept his gaze over the woods.

There was no sign of Abby.

He swallowed a sigh, not wanting to admit she'd gotten the better of him. Again. His previous admiration turned to full-blown annoyance. Why wouldn't she believe him? He hadn't threatened her or done anything to hurt her.

In his role as the lead FBI agent working on organized crime cases, he'd interacted with many scared witnesses, especially those testifying against terrifyingly brutal crime bosses. But none as skittish as Abby.

Should he head to his SUV? Or wait here a little longer?

The highway had remained deserted, but now he saw a faint glow in the distance to his right. He frowned, as the glow slowly grew brighter.

A car was coming toward him.

It would look suspicious if he continued crouching on the side of the sedan closest to the road, so he quickly rose off his knees and edged along the side of the car until he'd rounded the sedan, to take cover on the other side.

If Abby was watching from a safe spot in the woods, she'd likely see him. Yet, that was better than drawing attention from a stranger, who could easily call 911 to report a suspicious man hiding behind a car.

Twin headlights pierced the darkness. He had to turn his gaze away from the sudden brightness, wondering if the driver had his high beams on to better see any potential wildlife running out onto the road. On his ride in, he'd noticed more than one dead deer lying at the side of the road.

He expected the vehicle to fly past at highway speeds, but it didn't. The driver slowed, as if to look closely at the sedan.

A warning chill snaked down his spine. This was not a random driver passing through. As soon as the thought flashed in his mind, he noticed the vehicle slowing even further. Then gunfire reverberated through the night.

Windows shattered. Wyatt crouched lower behind the vehicle, making himself as small as possible, even as he felt the sedan behind him shift, lurching sideways. It took a moment for him to understand the shooter had taken out the tires while also attempting to kill anyone who might be behind the wheel.

No way did he think this was the work of bored kids with too much time on their hands. The shots had been carefully placed to render the vehicle undrivable.

Wyatt pulled his weapon from its holster, gripping it with both hands. The shooter in the car was too close now for him to make a run for it, so he flattened himself to the ground, edging beneath the underbelly of the sedan.

He hoped Abby stayed in the woods until he'd figured out what was going on.

The vehicle pulled over to the side of the road in front of Abby's useless sedan. He briefly considered shooting the tires that may have belonged to a truck, but then decided against it.

The driver must not have seen him, otherwise why would he pull over? Wyatt remained still, hoping to use the element of surprise to his advantage.

Unfortunately, he was too low to see the driver's face; all he could make out was the man's large, booted feet as he slid out from behind the wheel.

The shooter stood for a moment, the tips of his feet facing the woods. Wyatt imagined he was searching for a sign of his quarry. Suddenly, a loud thunk reached his ears, followed by a rock dropping from the side of the sedan to the ground a few inches from him.

He knew Abby had tossed the rock. A split second later, the gunman fired several shots toward the woods.

Wyatt fired back, hitting the guy's ankles. Not the most glamorous of shots, but it was enough to cause the shooter to howl in pain, dropping to the ground while clutching his leg.

Another second later, Wyatt became the target as the guy's gun turned toward him. Without hesitation, he fired again, hitting the gunman in the chest.

This time, the guy didn't shout in pain but fell limply back, lying lifeless on the ground just four feet away.

Wyatt didn't move for a long moment. Then he crawled out and stood, then approached the fallen man.

A person shot out of the woods, coming toward him. He instinctively raised his gun, then lowered it when he recognized Abby.

"Who is he?" She stared at the man lying dead on the ground. "I saw the whole thing— the way he shot out my windows and the tires, then looked as if he was going to come searching for me."

"I have no doubt he was searching for you." A shiver of apprehension washed over him as he stared at the dead man. "I've never seen him before." He knelt and patted his pockets, finding car keys, a wad of cash and a burner phone. "No ID."

"Do you think he's a professional hit man?" Abby asked.

"Yes. I'm certain of it." He hadn't anticipated a hit man coming after the Millers.

Yet it was clear that the goal here was to silence Abby and her father.

Permanently.

TWO

Abby shivered as she stared at the dead man. Then she looked up at Wyatt, the FBI agent who'd taken him out. While she was starting to believe he wasn't the shooter who'd tried to kill her father all those months ago, she still wasn't happy with how things had worked out. "The only way he could have found us is by following you."

Wyatt grimaced. "Or you. But assuming you're right, please know I'm on your side, Abby. Yours and your father's. I've taken a personal leave of absence from the Bureau, but Hawthorne could have had me followed. This guy—" he gestured to the dead man "—would have killed both of us without blinking an eye."

She hated to admit he was right. No matter whom the gunman had followed, his motive was impossible to ignore.

"Let's go. My SUV isn't far." Wyatt bent and retrieved the phone and the cash. Then he hesitated and took a moment to press the dead man's fingers against a business card, which he tucked into a baggie. He went a step further to take a close-up picture of the man's face with his phone.

"You're going to run his prints? Put his features through a facial recognition program?"

He glanced up at her. "I'm going to try to convince a local cop to do those things for me. Like I said, I don't trust anyone within the Bureau."

She frowned. "I'd rather not talk to the local cops."

"We won't do that now, but maybe later." He pocketed the items he'd taken from the dead man. "Will you come with me?"

Her car wasn't going anywhere, so she nodded. Wyatt hadn't threatened her with his gun, which made it more likely he was telling the truth. "But not until after I head back to the cabin, see if my dad shows up."

"We can't stay long," Wyatt warned. "This guy found us here. Others could, too."

Again, she hated to admit he was right. But she needed to check one more time. "Where exactly is your car?"

"Half mile up the road, just around the curve." He gestured with his hand, then added, "It's still a solid mile-long hike back to the cabin."

She hesitated, wondering if the detour was worth it. There was no evidence to prove her dad was staying there. And in the time it would take for them to go back and forth, another gunman might show up. Yet she couldn't abandon her father. "I'm sorry, but I need to go back. I've come too far not to see my dad."

To her surprise, Wyatt didn't argue. "Let's go."

She turned and led the way back across the clearing, until they'd reached the shelter of the woods. They'd only traveled a quarter mile when she realized Wyatt was limping.

"What happened?" she whispered.

He shook his head. "It's fine. Keep going."

She did, because there wasn't another option. But she slowed her pace a bit, listening intently.

When they reached the cabin, she noticed there was no longer any smoke coming from the chimney. Battling a wave of dismay, she rushed up to the back door and went inside.

The fire in the wood-burning stove had been put out. The log she'd thrown at Wyatt had been replaced on the wood pile.

Even as she quickly searched the bedrooms, she knew it was too late.

The occupant was gone.

Her father? Her gut told her yes, but without proof, she couldn't be sure. She stood for a moment in the center of the cabin, searching for something, anything that might offer a clue.

But found nothing.

Dejected, she turned to face Wyatt. "Let's hit the road. If my dad was here, he's not anymore."

Wyatt nodded and stepped back so she could precede him out the door. She glanced over her shoulder one last time, noting there was no electricity in the cabin for her dad to recharge his phone if the battery had died. One possible reason he hadn't answered her calls. Yet even as the thought crossed her mind, she knew there was something more going on here.

Something that had scared her father into cutting all ties with her.

When they were back in the woods, Wyatt stepped forward to take the lead. She didn't mind, her thoughts still whirling. If her father had been there, why not wait around until she returned? If he'd been keeping watch on the place, he'd have recognized her.

Had he stayed hidden out of sight because of Special Agent Wyatt Kane? Maybe.

She let out a heavy sigh. One good thing about the night's events: if her father had spent time here, then her plan to revisit their previous hiding places was on target.

A kernel of hope bloomed in her heart. She could head to the next location, the safe house they'd used before coming to this cabin in the woods. It would bring her closer to Green Lake, Wisconsin, where their run from the Marchese crime family had started eighteen years ago.

Her father had escaped his father and brother, Walter and Tony Marchese, because he hadn't wanted to be a member of their criminal organization, especially not when they'd tried to force him to kill a man. After leaving Chicago, he'd settled in Green Lake, finding safety and love within the Amish community. Her dad had married Arleta, her mother, and they'd had twin daughters, Rachel and Abby. But when the Marcheses found him living among the Amish, her dad had been forced to flee, taking Abby with him, leaving Rachel and her mother, behind. He hadn't done so on purpose. Her sister Rachel had been sick at home with her mother, while her dad had taken her with him to work in the field. When he'd recognized the Marchese hit man, he'd had little choice but to take off with Abby, leaving Rachel and her mother behind. At one point he tried to head back for the rest of his family, but realized the hit man had staked out the house. Forcing her father to take Abby, disappearing from the Amish community, forever.

Abby had only been four years old at the time and didn't have any memories about her life with the Amish. But despite that, her father had encouraged her to remember street names and other landmarks as they moved from place to place, hiding from danger.

Those memories helped her now.

The next location where her dad may be hiding was an old farmhouse on Duncan Lane, about two miles off highway ZZ. Granted, it was possible the house had been destroyed a long time ago. But she still needed to check it out.

She focused on following Wyatt's limping gait through the woods. He didn't utter a single complaint, which was admirable. And he didn't let his injury slow him down, either. When they finally reached the edge of the tree line, he stopped and held up a hand. Abby took refuge behind one tree, while he used another for cover. Ahead of them was the road, with an SUV parked on the shoulder.

Scanning the area, she didn't see anything out of the ordinary for the time being close to midnight.

Lights bloomed in the distance, and Wyatt dropped to his knee behind the tree. She mimicked his movement, watching closely at the vehicle that approached.

Thankfully, the car didn't slow down, but zoomed past. Still, Wyatt didn't move for a long time.

"Is that your personal SUV?" she asked in a whisper. "Or one provided by the FBI?"

He shook his head. "A rental obtained in Chicago. I used my own name, so there is a possibility it's been compromised. Stay here, I'm going to check it out."

Without waiting for a response, he pulled his weapon and ran lightly across the open field to the side of the road. He took his time inspecting the vehicle from all angles, even going as far to shimmy beneath the SUV on his back, flashing his phone at the undercarriage.

She was impressed by his thoroughness. Trusting him wasn't easy, but she was beginning to think he was in as much danger as she and her father were from his boss, Ethan Hawthorne.

"It's clear," he finally called.

Leaving the shelter of the trees, she hurried over to join him. He opened the passenger door for her, and she quickly hopped in. As she secured her seat belt, he slid behind the wheel.

They were on the road in less than a minute and despite sitting in an FBI agent's car, she found herself relaxing, especially when heat radiated from the vents.

"Where are we going?" She glanced at Wyatt. Now that she wasn't regarding him with keen suspicion, she could secretly admit he was handsome. For a fed.

"The closest motel." He sighed and rubbed the back of his neck. "We need time to regroup. Figure out our next steps."

She arched a brow. "*We*? We're a team now?"

"Yes." He scowled. "Did you forget about the gunman back there? The one who shot out your windows and tires, then aimed at you in the woods? We're both in danger, Abby, and so is your father."

"I haven't forgotten." She shifted in the seat. The issue wasn't the danger—it was the fact she'd grown accustomed to working alone.

Back in the spring she'd had a friend, Greg Sharma, helping her track the Marchese men. But Greg had been murdered, and since then, the only partner she'd had was her father. And even then, they'd gone their separate ways several times over the years. Especially when it became clear the Marcheses had learned about her father's twin daughters.

Abby hadn't given herself much time to

think about her twin, Rachel. They were identical in looks, but not in any other way. Rachel was Amish, dedicated to her community. Abby had no experience with the plain people, as she'd heard them called, other than the brief interaction when she'd helped rescue her twin from the Marchese family.

The one hobby they shared was cooking. Rachel had turned her skill into a business, opening her own restaurant, while Abby had worked in a variety of restaurants, as a cook more often than not. Thankfully, most restaurants didn't mind the gaps between her jobs, as hard workers were hard to come by.

Maybe someday she and Rachel would be able to visit again. She would like to stay in touch if that sort of thing was allowed by the Amish. She wasn't entirely sure what the rules were. Her dad had only mentioned that having left the Amish, he could never go back.

"There's a motel three miles from here." As Wyatt spoke, she saw the old worn billboard advertising the Willow Grove Motel.

"Okay." She sent him a quick glance. "I'd prefer my own room, though."

"I'll get two rooms," he agreed. "Hopefully they'll take cash."

"Sorry, but I don't have much cash on me," she admitted. Searching for her father had put a serious dent in her meager savings. "My plan was to head back to Green Lake to get a job in one of the local restaurants. I like to cook, and most restaurants are always looking for cooks or servers."

"I don't expect you to pay. I feel bad enough knowing I may have led the gunman to you."

She wasn't sure what to say to that. Wyatt's SUV ate up the miles and it wasn't long before he left the highway to pull up in front of the dilapidated Willow Grove Motel. He stared at it for a moment, then turned toward her. "Should I keep going? This place doesn't look great."

"I've stayed in worse." She shrugged. "Up to you. I think the next closest town is Green Lake."

He threw the gearshift into Park. "Let's see what they have. Wait for me here in the car. If it's not feasible for us to stay, we'll keep going."

She nodded and he quickly jumped out and headed inside. His limp wasn't as noticeable now, so maybe taking the pressure off had helped. Staring out the window, she wondered about her dad. Was he still back in the woods? Or had he headed off in the opposite direction on foot?

Useless to wish things had gone down differently at the cabin. She couldn't blame her dad for taking extra precautions. Or maybe the intruder hadn't been her father, at all. For all she knew, someone else owned the cabin. Although that did not explain why the occupant had taken off.

A wave of exhaustion hit her hard. She yawned, fighting the urge to close her eyes and lean her head against the window.

She'd never imagined teaming up with the FBI agent that her father believed had betrayed him. Her gut told her Wyatt wasn't the dirty cop her father had thought him to be.

She stared up at the dark sky, hoping she wasn't making a colossal mistake.

Convincing the owner of Willow Grove Motel to take cash for two connecting rooms wasn't difficult. Wyatt stressed that if the rooms were filthy or infested with bedbugs he'd be back for a refund.

The owner had assured him that the rooms were clean and pest-free. Wyatt hoped he was right.

Returning to the SUV, he held up two keys. "We have connecting rooms. Hope that's okay. It's safer to stick together."

"Good idea," Abby agreed.

He drove around to park along the side of

the building, rather than in the spaces directly in front of the doors. He gave Abby a key, then used the other to unlock his door.

The room wasn't the worst he'd ever been in, but the musty smell had him wrinkling his nose. He did a quick check of the bedding to make sure the place wasn't infested with bedbugs, then headed over to unlock his side of the connecting door.

He knocked and waited for her to open the door. "Sorry it's not that great," he apologized stepping across the threshold to join her. "But it's clean and the owner agreed to take cash, which was helpful. We'll hit the road first thing in the morning."

"It's fine." Thankfully, she didn't quibble over the accommodations. She gestured to his left leg. "Do you want me to look at your ankle?"

"No, I'm good. I'll ice it later." Wyatt pulled the cash and disposable phone he'd taken from the gunman. He quickly checked recent calls, but didn't find any. Not that he'd expected to, but it was worth a try. He set the items on the small table, then turned to face her. "I need to know where you think your dad will go next."

She dropped onto the edge of the bed. "I have a place in mind. It's not far from here, actually, but I'd like to go alone." When he began to protest, she stopped him. "My dad doesn't trust you, Wyatt. I need time to talk to him, let him know what's happened, okay?"

He struggled to control his frustration. "Okay, fine. I understand your dad's reticence. But I insist on being somewhere close by in case another gunman shows up."

She shrugged. "We'll find a place that's not too close, and not too far."

He drilled her with a narrow look. "Don't think of leaving without me, Abby. We need to stick together until we know exactly what we're up against."

"How am I going to leave without you? I don't have a car."

Somehow, he didn't think that fact alone would stop her. She was one of the most resourceful women he'd ever known. "I need you to trust me. I don't want anything to happen to you or your father."

"I know." She had the grace to look ashamed. "I'm sure I'll get used to working with a partner."

Her words made him think of his FBI partner, Allan Trudeau. His partner had undergone an unexpected hernia surgery and was off duty, so Wyatt hadn't expressed his concerns about Hawthorne, or the real reason behind his sudden need for a personal leave. Trudeau hadn't been involved in his discussions with Peter Miller, either, so there'd been no reason to drag Allan into his mess.

He considered calling Allan now, but then decided against it. His partner would want to follow protocol, which meant talking to their boss, and that wasn't happening. For now, Wyatt refused to use any of the FBI resources he would normally have at his fingertips.

Allan was probably back at work by now. Maybe at some point, when he had the proof he needed against Hawthorne, he'd call his partner.

But not yet.

"It's getting late." Rising to her feet, she glanced pointedly at the connecting door. "I need to get some rest. You should, too."

Oddly, he would have preferred to keep talking with her. Seeing her this close for the first time, he couldn't deny Abby was beautiful, right down to the small mole on the corner of her mouth. Not that he was interested in her on a personal level, he quickly reminded himself. That was a nonstarter.

His career had destroyed one relationship, and his former fiancée had stomped on his heart when she'd left him.

No way was he willing to risk getting hurt like that again.

His job as an FBI agent working on organized crime cases required travel, and he couldn't discuss all aspects of his work, either. Earlier this year Emma had given him an ultimatum: his job or her. Of course, he'd wanted her, so he'd prepared to give his notice to the Bureau. But then he'd gotten the phone call from Peter Miller on a day his boss wasn't in. Normally, any sources providing inside information went to Hawthorne first before being given to specific agents. He'd notified Hawthorne after their first meeting, thrilled to work with Miller; getting intel on the Marchese crime family was a big deal. Something they'd been working on for years.

Wyatt hadn't been able to walk away. He'd begged Emma to give him more time, but she'd flat-out refused. She'd kept the engagement ring and stormed out.

He hadn't seen her since. And really, it was easier to stay focused on his job without her whining about how much time he spent working. He'd honestly tried to spend time with Emma, taking her on surprise trips, nice dinners, even an impromptu vacation to Aruba, but nothing had been good enough.

Now that he was in danger, he was doubly

glad Emma had left when she did. One less thing to worry about. He focused on the present. "Getting sleep sounds like a plan. We'll regroup in the morning. Good night, Abby." He turned away to cross the threshold between their connecting doors.

"Good night." Her soft, husky voice floated after him.

A wave of attraction caught him off guard. He quickly shook it off. This wasn't the time or place to be aware of a woman. He told himself he needed to stay focused on the threat that loomed over them.

He washed up in the bathroom, then went out to grab some ice from the machine located around the corner from Abby's room. Stretching out on the bed, he made an ice pack with a towel, wrapping it around his injured ankle.

Despite his physical exhaustion, his thoughts whirled. Pulling out his phone, he brought up the photograph of the shooter's face.

The guy looked slightly familiar, but Wyatt couldn't place him. He tried to think through the known mafia associates he had in his files. Maybe he was a sibling of one of them? Either way, there was no doubt in his mind that this dead guy had been hired by Hawthorne to kill Abby and her father.

The leak within the FBI had to be Hawthorne. He'd only told his boss about the second meeting with Miller, no one else knew about it. And the way Hawthorne had turned on Wyatt, accusing him of being the leak only added credence to his theory.

The fact Wyatt had been on Abby's trail, too, had likely played right into Hawthorne's plan. If his presence had been discovered, his boss would have set Wyatt up as the bad guy, pinning the murders of Abby and her father on him.

Tying the case up in a neat little bow.

Abby didn't want to interact with the local law enforcement, but he needed to find a way to identify the gunman. Wyatt felt certain that if he dug deep enough he'd find the attacker's link to Hawthorne, even if the guy was nothing but a thug for hire.

Or a connection to the Marchese family.

Walter Marchese was the founding father of the crime family, but he was in a facility with Alzheimer's disease. His son Tony Marchese and Tony's cousin, Franco, were both in federal custody. Franco initially had blabbed to the local cops, eager to place all blame for their criminal activities on Tony. Then he'd abruptly stopped cooperating. Wyatt had assumed Tony had threatened Franco to keep him quiet. And strangely enough, Franco never mentioned having an inside source within the FBI.

Because Franco didn't know about Hawthorne? Maybe. Tony was smart, and may have kept that information to himself.

Wyatt had tried to visit them in prison, only to find he was banned by his own boss from speaking to them. When he'd confronted Hawthorne, his boss had told him he'd been removed from the case because the "higher-ups" would be taking over the interview.

More likely, Hawthorne himself had gone to speak to them, pressuring the two to remain silent while promising to get them out.

As if that was happening.

Yet even the remote possibility of his boss coming up with something to free either man had been enough for him to take his leave of absence to work the case on his own. Starting with finding Peter Miller as a potential witness

And if he was caught working as an agent while on leave from the Bureau?

He could kiss his career goodbye.

Better that, than to end up dead, he thought grimly. Setting his phone aside, he closed his eyes for a moment. He'd been raised to believe in God, although his faith had stumbled when Emma had left him.

But since everything had gone sideways, especially after a gunman showed up at his meeting with Peter Miller, nearly killing the guy, he'd leaned heavily on prayer to get him through.

He did the same thing now. Praying for the strength and wisdom to bring those who'd committed these terrible crimes to justice.

A ringing sound drew him from slumber. Wyatt bolted upright, grabbing his phone. But when he blinked the sleep from his eyes, he realized the sound wasn't coming from his device.

Abby's? He stood, forgetting about his injured ankle, to rush through their connecting rooms.

Then stopped, when he saw Abby was sitting on the edge of the bed, staring at the small table he'd used earlier.

The gunman's phone was ringing.

He crossed over and picked it up. After pressing the accept call button, he brought the device to his ear.

"Yeah?" He used a low, rough voice to answer.

A momentary pause, then, "Is it done?"

The voice was a subdued whisper, making it almost impossible to match it with either Hawthorne or anyone else within the Bureau.

"Yes." He locked gazes with Abby as he played along. "Both the man and the woman are dead."

Another long pause, then the line abruptly disconnected. He tried to call the number back, but received an error message stating the line was no longer in service. He frowned, trying to understand what had just happened.

"Who was that?" Abby asked.

He shook his head. "I'm not sure, but whatever I said must have tipped him off that I wasn't the gunman." He thought back, wondering what had gone wrong. "I said the man and the woman were dead, meaning you and your father. Maybe he was only supposed to kill you, Abby."

She paled. "Do you think he recognized your voice wasn't right?"

"That's a possibility, too. Or he expected me to use your names." He stared at the disposable phone. The only thing he could say for certain was that the gunman had been hired to kill Abby.

But who had paid him? The FBI?

Or someone else?

Either way, he had a very bad feeling the attempts wouldn't stop until the job was done.

THREE

The ringing phone had jolted Abby from sleep. She'd instinctively reached for her device, hoping the caller was her father.

Instead, it was the gunman's phone that had gone off. Listening to Wyatt trying to assure the caller the mission had been accomplished sent a chill down her spine.

She'd known the gunman had intended to kill her. Yet hearing the blunt words had been unnerving. She had to give Wyatt credit for playing along to get more information.

"Did you recognize the caller's voice?" She stared at Wyatt through the darkness. Some moonlight filtered through the curtains, so she could see his concerned expression.

"No." He set the device down on the table. "The guy spoke in a hushed whisper, so I can't honestly say the caller was my boss, Ethan Hawthorne. To be fair, anyone could have hired the gunman."

She held his gaze for a long moment. "I'm glad you're not the mole working for the Marchese family." Of course, his shooting the gunman had been a big clue, too, but deep down it was difficult to let go of a belief she and her father had held for the past ten months.

"I told you I only followed you to find your father, to get evidence that can help bring down the dirty FBI agent." There was a hard edge to his tone. "I'm as much of a target now as you are."

"I know." She grimaced. "It's just that the attempt to kill my dad happened right before his meeting with you."

"I'm aware." Wyatt said tersely. "I'm pretty sure my boss set me up to take the fall. He's the only one who knew about my second meeting with your father. The one that ended with an attempt to kill him."

"Why would Hawthorne want to kill me and my dad now that the Marcheses are in jail?"

He dropped into the chair next to the table. "I think he's worried the Marcheses will talk. Especially since Franco was blabbing at first, then abruptly stopped cooperating. I'm sure Hawthorne is keeping them quiet by promising them a way out. But there's another possibility, too." His expression turned grim. "It could be they aren't the only crime family Hawthorne is working with."

"Another crime family?" She shouldn't have been surprised. At twenty-three, she'd met more than her fair share of criminals. "Who?"

Wyatt stared gloomily at the gunman's phone without answering for a long moment. "I guess I can tell you since I'm not working this case on an official level." He sighed and rubbed the back of his neck. "Have you heard of the Raffa family? Headed by Johnny Raffa?"

She frowned. "No, should I have heard of them?"

"My job in the Bureau is to work organized crime cases. Johnny Raffa is trying to take over whatever business is left of the Marchese empire. It's possible Raffa has Hawthorne on his payroll, too."

Again, she shouldn't be surprised by the news. "I would think the Marcheses would spill the beans on Hawthorne without blinking an eye, especially if they knew Johnny Raffa was taking over their business."

"That was my hope, but so far, they haven't. After Franco's arrest, he blamed everything on Tony without mentioning anything about a source within the FBI. I figure the Raffas might want to keep that insider connection, too." He grimaced. "I was hoping your dad had more information to give me on the Marcheses' business ventures that may tie into whatever the Raffa family and my boss are doing now."

She shook her head. "You must understand that my father's information is not current. He escaped his father and his uncle years ago to avoid being dragged into the criminal structure they were building. I know he reached out to you to provide inside information, but that was an effort to keep us both safe as the Marcheses had renewed their efforts to find us." She frowned. "Instead, he put us both in danger."

"I know, and I'm truly sorry about that." Wyatt's features turned stern. "Your father is all I have, Abby. Without his help, Hawthorne will continue to allow Raffa and the other organized crime families to continue their illegal business as usual."

That was a lot to expect from her father, but she understood Wyatt's frustration. "Or we find a way to convince the Marcheses to turn on your boss."

"Not an easy task since they've recently refused to speak to anyone but their lawyer."

"Maybe we should talk to their lawyer. Explain your suspicions about your boss. Let the lawyer know that if the Marcheses turn on Hawthorne, they may be eligible for a lesser sentence. If that's something you can offer."

Admiration flashed in his eyes. "It's a really good idea, although I'd have to get someone else in the higher ranks of the Bureau to back my plan. I'm not sure who to trust, but it's worth a try. The law firm is in Chicago." Wyatt reached for his phone and poked at the screen. "Their lawyer's name is Jerome Gardner." He used the device for a few minutes. "Okay, here it is. The law firm of Gardner and Twain is located in downtown Chicago."

Chicago was a good five-hour drive from their current location. Traffic would be a giant snarl by the time they reached the city. "How soon can we head to Chicago?" She was glad he'd taken her suggestion of talking to the Marchese lawyer to heart if he could find someone higher up to approve the arrangement. Before they left town, though, she wanted to stop by the Green Lake property to see if her father was there.

"Not yet. I need to think long and hard about who I can trust at the Bureau. We also need to look for your father." He slowly rose and took a step toward the connecting door.

"I don't want anything to happen to your dad, Abby. It would be best if he teamed up with the two of us."

She agreed, but they had to find him, first. "I know. Me, either. Good night, Wyatt."

"Good night." He disappeared into his room.

Abby tried to go back to sleep, but questions whirled in her mind. Did her father know anything relevant about the Marchese business dealings that would help Wyatt prove his boss was dirty?

And what about Johnny Raffa? While it was interesting the guy was taking over the Marchese family activities, there was no reason for Raffa to come after her or her dad.

If she had a smartphone, she'd look him up, but all she owned was the disposable one that she didn't dare give up, as it was the only link she had with her father.

Where are you, Dad? She stared up at the ceiling, trying to imagine her father sneaking away from the cabin in the woods, and finding a way to meet with her at the house on Duncan Lane. She only needed five minutes to convince him that Wyatt Kane wasn't the bad guy in all of this. She was sure her father would join them in bringing down the FBI mole.

She sighed and turned on her side, doing her best to relax enough to get some sleep.

The next thing Abby knew, sunlight drew her awake. She blinked and pushed herself upright. The hour was going on seven thirty in the morning. After cleaning up in the bathroom, she hesitantly approached the connecting doorway between their rooms.

"Wyatt? Are you in there?"

"Yes." He met her in the doorway, his limp much improved. "Are you hungry? We can stop for breakfast along the way."

"That would be great." She hadn't eaten dinner last night, and her stomach was growling loud enough she feared he'd hear it. "You didn't see any other vehicles near the cabin, did you?"

"No, why?"

She grimaced. "I'm not sure how my dad will get to the next meeting place, especially if he doesn't have a car."

"I see." Wyatt looked thoughtful. "Maybe we can make a stop in Green Lake. I was hoping to convince one of the cops there to help run the fingerprints I picked up through the system."

"That should work. I know I said I didn't want the locals involved, but Sheriff Liam Harland seems like a decent guy. He's the

one who took Franco and Tony into custody."
Her interaction with the Green Lake sheriff
had been minimal, but her twin Rachel had
nothing but nice things to say about him a few
months ago, when she'd helped save her sister's life. Abby herself hadn't stayed around
long enough to find out.

"Great." He brightened. "I'm glad to hear
that. Let's hit the road."

Abby followed Wyatt outside and around
the corner of the motel building where he'd
left his SUV. As he drove, he used the GPS
built into the vehicle to pull up local restaurants.

"Looks like there are a few places to eat
before we get to Green Lake. There's a family restaurant just a mile away."

"That works." She thought briefly about
her twin sister's restaurant in Green Lake,
it would be great to see her again, but it was
best to avoid Rachel now. The last thing she
wanted was for her twin to be in danger again
because of the Marchese crime family.

Once she found her father, and the threat
was over, she'd take her dad to Rachel's Café
to reunite the family. But until then, she
needed to stay far away.

The restaurant they stopped in wasn't very
busy. She noticed Wyatt chose a table in the

corner, far from the scattered customers who were already seated.

"Coffee?" A pleasant woman in her mid-forties brought two mugs and a pot of coffee.

"Yes, please," she and Wyatt said at the exact same time.

The woman laughed and proceeded to fill their mugs. "My name is Clare. Cream and sugar are on the table, I'll give you a few minutes to look at the menu."

"Thanks." Wyatt took a sip of his black coffee, while she doctored hers with cream and sugar. When they were alone again, he said, "I'm ready to order whenever you are."

"Really?" She eyed him curiously. "Come here often?"

"No, but I like the standard breakfast." He shrugged, looking slightly embarrassed. "Creature of habit."

Moments later, they placed their order. She surreptitiously pulled out her disposable phone to check for any missed calls from her father.

There were none.

"When we finish here, we'll head to the sheriff's department," Wyatt said. "How long do we give your dad to show at the house?"

"I don't know." She slipped the phone back in her pocket. "You could always leave me at the house while you head to Green Lake to talk to the sheriff."

"No." He stared at her with intense green eyes. "We're sticking together, Abby."

She sipped her coffee, then nodded. "Okay, fine. But that will delay your investigation."

"It can't be helped." A frown furrowed his brow. "I don't like knowing your father is in danger."

"I appreciate that." She set her coffee aside as Clare returned with their meals. She picked up her fork, then hesitated when she noticed Wyatt had bowed his head to pray.

Her father used to do that when she was young. Then, over the years, he'd strayed from the habit. She'd thought his praying was a holdover from his time with the Amish, but here Wyatt was proving her wrong. It wasn't just the Amish who prayed before meals. Regular people, even an FBI agent, did.

She set her fork down and bowed her head, too.

"Lord, bless this food we are about to eat," Wyatt said in a low voice. "And keep us safe in Your care. Amen."

"Amen." She lifted her head to meet his gaze. "That was nice."

"We're going to need God's strength to get

through this." He offered a wry smile. "But I'm confident we'll succeed."

Abby picked up her fork and took a bite of her eggs, hoping he was right about that.

She desperately needed to believe she and her dad would survive this, too.

Wyatt dug into his meal, energized by both their plan for the day and the way Abby had prayed with him. Granted, Abby may be simply going through the motions, the way Emma had, but that was okay. It wasn't as if they'd be together forever.

This was a temporary partnership, just long enough to bring Hawthorne to justice.

Deep down, Wyatt knew that his career would not survive this. Even if he was able to prove Hawthorne's guilt, working the case on his own may be enough for the leadership within the Bureau to cut him loose.

And if that happened? He'd deal with it. No way was he going to let the possibility of losing his job stop him. Especially since his reputation was tarnished anyway thanks to Hawthorne throwing suspicion on him, deflecting it from himself.

He watched Abby as they ate. Her offer to stay behind bothered him. She'd insisted on going to meet with her father alone, although he planned to be someplace nearby. Yet it made him wonder if she was planning to take off with her father, leaving him to deal with the mess of the Marchese and Raffa families on his own.

In a way, he could understand why she'd be tempted to go with her father, dropping off grid once again. Peter had tried to do the right thing in helping the Feds find and arrest the Marchese family.

Narrowly escaping a murder attempt for his efforts.

Abby finished her meal first. He arched a brow. "Would you like something more?"

"Oh, no thanks." She blushed. "I missed dinner, but I'm fine now."

For the first time, he wondered how she and her father had been getting by. "Do you need money? I can give you some."

"I'm good for now." She didn't meet his gaze. "I was planning to pick up a job in Green Lake, but that can wait."

He made a mental note to make sure she and Peter had what they needed, cash and reliable transportation once this was over. It was the least he could do. He quickly finished his meal, then signaled for the bill.

Five minutes later, they were back on the road. His GPS told him they were fifteen miles from Green Lake, which would put them at the Sheriff's Department at roughly nine in the morning.

As he navigated the curvy roads, he kept a wary eye on his rearview mirror. He didn't see anything resembling a tail, but then again, he hadn't noticed one last night, either. Somehow, the shooter had arrived on the scene, anyway.

And the caller on the disposable phone had wanted to know if it was done.

He'd chosen to take less traveled roads into Green Lake, although as they grew closer to the town, the ability to avoid being followed diminished greatly. Stunning red, yellow and orange fall colors brightened the trees, bringing tourists flocking to the area. They were soon surrounded by other cars.

"Would you mind turning right at the next intersection?" Abby asked.

"I don't mind, but is there something you're looking for in particular?"

"We're fairly close to the area where my dad may be headed," she admitted. "I thought we could do a quick drive-by, see if the structure is even still there."

"Okay." He did as she asked, then turned left on a narrow road that looked as if no one had driven on it in decades. The asphalt was buckled in several areas, revealing large cracks that allowed weeds to grow tall enough to brush the underside of his SUV.

It didn't look as if a vehicle had gone this way in a very long time.

"Up ahead." Abby gestured to the right. "There should be a driveway."

"An overgrown one, I'm sure," he said wryly. But when he noticed a very narrow opening between two towering trees, he turned in.

Again, the driveway hadn't been used in months, maybe years. As the drive grew more rocky, he stopped.

"Might be better to go the rest of the way on foot."

"It looks different from what I remember." Abby pushed her door open and stepped out. "I thought the house would be right over there." She gestured to an area up ahead.

Even though there was no sign of anyone lurking nearby, he pulled his weapon and led the way. They'd only gone maybe twenty yards, when he abruptly stopped.

The house, or what was left of it, was a pile of splintered and charred wood. The roof was almost completely gone except for about one quarter of the structure, and only some of the walls remained.

"Oh no!" Abby stared in horror. "It's been destroyed by a fire."

"Yeah." He couldn't tell if the fire had been the result of lightning, simple carelessness, or arson. The reason the place had burned didn't matter.

Peter Miller wasn't hiding out here, that was for sure.

Abby sighed and turned away from the ruin. "I'll still come back later, in case my dad shows up."

He batted down a flash of impatience. Their time may well be better spent heading to Chicago after talking to the sheriff in Green Lake, but he told himself if there was even a remote chance of Peter showing up here, they needed to check back as she'd suggested.

"Okay, that's fine. For now, we'll keep with the plan of chatting with Sheriff Harland." He turned and led the way back to the SUV.

Abby looked dejected as they began the jerky and jarring ride back to highway ZZ. As soon as they were off Duncan Lane, he hit the gas to get up to the speed limit.

Abby remained silent for several long moments. "How long ago do you think that fire took place?"

He shook his head. "I have no idea. That's not my area of expertise."

She grimaced. "I was really hoping my dad and I could use it as a hideout for a while."

He shot her a surprised look. "Why on earth would you do that? I thought the plan was for us to stick together."

There was a pause before she admitted, "Yes, it is. But Chicago is where this all started for my dad. First when he escaped his family, then earlier this year when he was almost killed while heading to your designated meeting place. I'm not sure he'll be thrilled about going back."

He swallowed his annoyance, trying to understand the situation from her point of view. He was about to reassure her when he noticed a car coming up fast on the highway behind him.

Not a car but a black truck, much like the one the shooter had been driving the night before.

"Wyatt?" Abby's tone registered alarm.

"Hang on." Thankfully, they were both wearing their seat belts. He punched the gas. The SUV leaped forward, putting some badly needed distance between them and the truck.

"How could the bad guys have followed us?" Abby asked, clinging to the door handle as he took the curves in the highway at breakneck speed.

"Don't know. Call 911."

She fumbled for her phone to do as he asked. He heard her make the call, while doing everything possible to lose the truck. No matter how fast he took the curves, the truck kept pace behind him.

They were still five miles from Green Lake. He seriously needed to lose this guy!

As he worked hard to keep the SUV on the road, a crack of gunfire came from the truck behind him, shattering the rear window.

FOUR

"Where are you currently located?" The 911 operator's calm voice helped keep her steady.

"South on highway ZZ heading toward Green Lake." Cold air blew around them from the broken rear window. Wyatt had his foot to the floor, the SUV careening down the road. A large black truck was visible in the side mirror. "The truck is gaining on us. Please, hurry!"

"I'll send a deputy to your location," the dispatcher said. "Is anyone hurt?"

Abby glanced at Wyatt's tense features as he put more distance between them and the black truck. She was about to reassure the dispatcher they weren't hurt yet when he abruptly swerved to the left. She fell partially against the passenger door, as far as the seat belt would allow, the phone flying from her fingers.

"I dropped the phone!" The shoulder harness was so tight she couldn't bend forward to search for it.

"Let it be, just hold on." Wyatt took another hard turn, the SUV rocking wildly as he did so.

Abby found herself whispering a prayer for God to keep them safe, which was strange because she didn't normally pray. Yet the plea came easily, and she knew her father would have done the same if he were here.

Glancing at the side mirror, she searched for signs the gunman's black truck was still behind them, but she couldn't see anything. Twisting in her seat, she shot a quick glance over her shoulder. The highway behind their SUV was empty. Despite the way they'd lost the gunman, Wyatt didn't slow down.

"Are you okay?" he asked tersely.

She managed a nod. "Yes, you?"

"Fine. But I want to know how we were picked up so quickly." His voice was grim. "I have to assume Hawthorne is tracking my phone since I haven't used my credit card since leasing the car." He sighed heavily, running his fingers through his hair. "We'll need to acquire another vehicle, ASAP."

It was staggering how extensively FBI resources were likely being used to find them. The way things had escalated so quickly made her wonder if they'd ever be safe. The only bright side was that she knew how to stay off grid. And that would mean using cash and disposable phones from this point forward.

A sign for Green Lake caught her attention. "We're almost there."

Before Wyatt could respond, she saw flashing red and blue lights approaching from the highway up ahead, wailing sirens splitting the air. She let out a silent sigh of relief, knowing the gunman would likely drop back even further behind now.

"Glad to see the deputies." Wyatt eased off the accelerator, breathing out a sigh of relief, as well. "That was way too close."

Her mouth was dry, and all she could do was nod. This skirmish with the assailant could have been much worse. A thought popped into her mind. "Wait a minute. Do you think they were tracking the gunman's disposable phone?"

Wyatt glanced at her with admiration. "I was just going to suggest that possibility, too." Then he frowned. "I should have ditched the phone, rather than bringing it to the motel."

"There's no way you could have anticipated this," she protested. It bothered her that he was blaming himself. "Especially since we eliminated the first threat on the highway near the cabin. And we can give the phone to the deputies now that they're on scene."

"Yeah, but if we're going to get to the bottom of this mess, I need to stay three steps ahead of my boss. Don't worry, I'll ditch my own phone soon enough." His words were difficult to hear above the screaming sirens. Wyatt pulled over to the side of the road and flipped on his hazard lights.

Then he surprised her by reaching over to take her hand. "I'm glad you weren't hurt, Abby."

She felt strangely breathless at the warmth of his fingers surrounding hers. "I—uh, ditto."

A smile kicked up the corner of his mouth, as the deputy squads pulled up alongside them. Wyatt released her to push open his door. She noticed he kept his hands in view as he stood. "I'm Special Agent Wyatt Kane with the FBI. The gunman was driving a black Ram truck, the first few digits on the license plate are 5-6-2."

She was impressed he'd gotten anything on the truck considering they were under fire. Following his lead, she slid out of the passenger door and came around to join him.

"Chief Deputy Garrett Nichols," the taller

of the two said. She remembered him from when she'd helped her twin, Rachel, escape being held at gunpoint by Tony Marchese.

Back when she'd thought the danger from the Marchese family was over.

The attacker finding the cabin and the recently shattered rear window of the SUV proved otherwise.

"I remember you," Nichols said, pinning Abby with an intense gaze. "You're Rachel's twin sister."

"Yes." Wyatt's eyes widened in surprise as she added, "I'm Abby Miller, and I'm working with Agent Kane to find my—er, our father." It was confusing as Nichols knew Rachel better than she did.

"Can we get somewhere safe before we talk any further?" Wyatt asked. "I don't like being out in the open like this."

Deputy Nichols glanced at his colleague, then nodded. "That sounds good to me. We'll escort you to our headquarters. It's not far."

"Good." Wyatt didn't argue, his gaze sweeping the area around them. "Let's go."

Abby quickly jumped back inside the SUV. Keeping his promise, Deputy Nichols pulled out first. Wyatt followed and the second deputy fell into place behind them. The three vehicles stayed together like cars on a train, all the way to downtown Green Lake.

The familiar landscape gave her a twinge. Abby and her father had traveled from one place to the next for so long that she didn't consider any of their temporary living arrangements as home.

But she had to admit Green Lake was the closest thing to a homelike atmosphere. Maybe because her sister lived there.

She shook off the sentiment as Wyatt parked in the lot located behind the building. Both deputies climbed out of their respective vehicles to escort them inside. It didn't take long for Deputy Nichols to take them to an interview room.

"Coffee or water?" Nichols asked.

"Water would be good," she said.

"Make that two," Wyatt added.

When they were alone, she leaned over, keeping her voice low. "How much are you going to tell them?"

He looked at her for a long moment. "This is no time to skirt the truth. I'll have to be honest about everything that's transpired, while imploring them not to go to my boss."

She swallowed hard. "What if they do?"

Wyatt shook his head. "That would not be good."

Before she could respond, the door opened and two men strode in. Nichols set two bottles of water on the table, then both men sat across from her and Wyatt.

"Sheriff Liam Harland," the newcomer introduced himself. "Garrett tells me you're Special Agent Wyatt Kane. Abby, I remember Rachel telling me about you from the incident last May. I have to say, I was not happy that you left without talking to us."

She winced and took a sip of her water. "Yes, I know. I'm very sorry about that, but you must know that I left because I needed to find my father."

Liam held her gaze. "I'd hoped you'd come back to speak with Rachel at the very least."

Mentioning her twin was like a punch to the gut. "I wanted to, but unfortunately things didn't go as planned. I thought the threat to me and my father was over. Turns out I was wrong." She hesitated, then asked, "How is Rachel? Is she happy?"

Liam nodded. "She is great, and very happily married to Jacob Strauss."

"Really?" She couldn't help but smile, remembering the tall Amish man who'd ridden to Rachel's rescue like a knight on a horse, throwing himself into the line of fire to save her twin. "I'm so glad to hear that."

She wished she could spend some time with Rachel, but not now.

Not while danger dogged their heels.

But once this was over, she silently promised to bring her father to visit with Rachel.

"Okay, let's get to the reason you're here," Liam said, turning his attention to Wyatt. "What's going on?"

"Sheriff, I need your assistance on this case I'm working." Wyatt held Liam's gaze for a long moment. "Before we start, I need assurances that you and Garrett will keep our conversation confidential."

Liam and Garrett frowned. "That depends on what you have to say," Liam drawled.

Wyatt shook his head. "I'm sorry, but that point isn't negotiable. This case is highly sensitive, and there may be a leak inside the FBI. I cannot give you anything unless you agree to abide by my wishes."

A long silence hung in the room. After what seemed like forever, Wyatt rose. "I'm sorry we can't stay. Abby and her father are in extreme danger. I appreciate your help getting us here, safely."

Abby couldn't believe Wyatt was just going to leave. As she rose to her feet, Liam waved a hand.

"Sit down, both of you. Garrett and I will

keep this conversation confidential, but I expect you to be honest about any threat heading into Green Lake. This is my county and I'm honor bound to protect the people living and vacationing here from harm." Liam narrowed his gaze. "And that is also nonnegotiable."

To her surprise, Wyatt grinned and returned to his seat. "Sounds good to me."

Abby also dropped back down, watching the three men closely. Bringing in the local law enforcement went against the grain; she and her father hadn't trusted anyone in years. Especially after the shooting attempt they'd believed to be the work of Agent Kane.

But she secretly admired how Wyatt held his own with the sheriff and chief deputy. She desperately wanted to believe trusting these men wouldn't come back to hurt them in the end.

And she really wanted this interview over so they could get back to the most important business of all.

Finding her father.

Trusting his instincts had gotten him this far, but Wyatt only hoped that he wasn't making a mistake in talking to Garrett and Liam. To their credit, they didn't interrupt as he explained how Peter Miller had called the organized crime division of the FBI and spoken with Wyatt in March of that year. He discussed how Peter had been very skittish about talking to him, and that he'd only given him a little bit of information about the Marchese business ventures at their first meeting. And how the gunfire at the location of their second meeting had ended all contact between them. He described his desire to find Peter Miller and how he'd followed Abby to the cabin in the woods to get her help. He finally ended the story with the gunman who'd shown up near the cabin, and the most recent gunfire targeting them on highway ZZ. He pulled the disposable phone he'd taken from the gunman and pushed it across the table.

"I answered a call, and a whispered voice asked if it was done. Clearly the guy intended to kill us."

Liam let out a deep breath and nodded. "Okay, I understand your concerns about a possible leak within the Bureau, but Franco and Tony Marchese were arrested in May. Why is there still a gunman following you now?"

"I'm technically working the case on my own," he was forced to admit. "And I know that sounds outlandish, but until I can make sure that both Peter and Abby are safe, I don't dare go to my superiors."

"What about someone who isn't within the organized crime division?" Garrett asked. "They can't all be dirty."

"No, they can't. The problem is that my boss, Ethan Hawthorne, has accused me of being the leak. He's putting all the blame of his actions onto me." This part was difficult to admit. "To be frank, my name is mud within the Bureau at the moment."

Liam grimaced. "I see the problem."

So far, the local cops had listened without bias. Since the entire discussion was going better than he'd hoped, Wyatt pulled out the plastic baggie holding the business card. "I have the dead gunman's prints on this. I was hoping you'd run them through AFIS." AFIS was the automated fingerprint identification system, and he hoped the prints were in the system. Most hired guns had a criminal background of some sort.

Garrett glanced at Liam, who nodded. "Go ahead and get them processed."

"Oh, I have a picture of the dead guy, too." He swiped through his phone until he found the photo, then slid it to Liam. "It may be enough to put through the facial recognition system, too."

Liam took the phone and stared at the photo for a long moment. "He doesn't look familiar, but I can ask my deputies if they've seen him. Can't hurt to put it through the system."

"Thank you." Wyatt gestured at the device. "When you're finished, please destroy the phone. I think my boss may be tracking it."

Liam's expression turned grim. "This is some mess you're in, Agent Kane."

"Please call me Wyatt, and I know." He glanced at Abby. "Once we find Peter and make sure he and Abby are safe, I plan to get to the bottom of this."

"I can help locally but don't have jurisdiction outside Green Lake County," Liam said.

"I appreciate that." He shrugged and added, "To be honest we'll have to head to Chicago very soon. That's where the Marchese organization was located, and that's where my boss is, too."

"Do you trust the Chicago PD?" Liam asked.

"No. I have learned that the mafia tends to buy local police to look the other way so they can continue breaking the law. I've considered contacting Chief of Police Rex Jericho, but it's hard to know which of his cops are dirty. Besides, my name isn't going to carry much weight right now." He lifted his hands.

"I may have to trust them at some point, but not today."

"Okay, why don't you both wait here while we deal with the evidence?" Liam stood, holding Wyatt's phone. "Maybe we'll be able to provide more information for you to use in the investigation."

"Thanks, Liam." Wyatt held the sheriff's gaze for a long moment. His gut told him he could trust Liam and Garrett, even if they couldn't help him in Chicago. "I appreciate everything you're doing for us."

Liam smiled and nodded. "Abby helped us arrest both Franco and Tony Marchese. It's only fair that we return the favor."

After Liam left, he turned to Abby. "I knew the Marcheses were captured and arrested, but what exactly was your role in that? Sounds like you were instrumental in bringing them to justice."

She blushed and shrugged. "Oh, it was nothing really. I did help, but so did my twin sister, Rachel. It's kind of a long story. We can talk about it later."

He sincerely doubted it was nothing and planned to hold her to that promise to explain.

Glancing at his watch, he sipped his water. The morning was still young, but he had several things they needed to do before they could leave. First thing on the list was to secure a replacement vehicle. One that had no ties to his name.

The idea of Hawthorne tracking his phone and finding them in Green Lake wouldn't leave him alone. Abby had also mentioned the possibility of the gunman's phone being tracked, but he was convinced his boss was involved.

In his mind, all roads led back to the Chicago FBI office of organized crime. Disheartening, to say the least.

"Hey, are you okay?" Abby rested her hand on his arm as if sensing his turmoil.

He forced a smile. "Yeah, I'm fine. We're safe here, even though we can't stay. We made the right decision to trust Liam and Garrett. The fact that they were instrumental in bringing Franco and Tony Marchese to justice helps."

"I know Rachel trusted them, too."

Liam poked his head into the room. "Garrett is still working on your evidence. Do you need anything else?"

"I know Franco Marchese spoke to you during your interrogation. Are you sure he didn't mention anything about having an inside track to the FBI?"

Liam came all the way in and shut the door

behind him. "He never said anything about the FBI. He claimed Tony was in charge and that he was only following Tony's orders. He also gave us names and addresses of several of the mafia business interests in Chicago."

"Will you share that list with me?"

Liam frowned. "I did share it with the FBI back in May. Didn't you see it?"

Anger burned in his belly. "No, I didn't. Hawthorne must have kept that tidbit of information to himself."

Liam whistled under his breath. "That's a problem. Hang tight, I'll dig that up while Garrett finishes running the prints and facial recognition."

"Thanks." After Liam left, he smacked his palm on the table. "I can't believe it! I wonder what other evidence Hawthorne kept from me?"

"Hey, you'll get what you need now," Abby said, her voice reassuring. "And you're smart, Wyatt. You'll find a way to prove your boss is a crook."

He hoped she was right, but it felt as if he was a blind man stumbling through the dark.

One thing was for sure: this only gave credence to his belief that Hawthorne was the leak within the Bureau. It was something he could use when it was time to go over Haw-thorne's head to the upper brass.

"Here you go." Liam entered the room. To Wyatt's surprise, the sheriff set a thick pile of paperwork on the table in front of him. "I made an entire copy of the Franco Marchese interview transcript."

"You did?" He felt as if he'd been given an early Christmas gift. He rested his palm on the stack of paper, wishing he could dive into it right now. "Thank you, Liam. This will help more than you know."

"I'm trusting you to do what's right," Liam said, a slight frown in his brow. "Normally, I'd vet you with the FBI office before giving you access to key and confidential informa-tion. But knowing what Abby and her father have been through, I've decided to trust your instincts about your boss. And I really want to make sure the people here in Green Lake are safe."

"I appreciate that," he said somberly. "Thank you."

The door opened to reveal Garrett Nich-ols, his expression full of satisfaction. "I got a hit on the prints and that matched the facial recognition."

He straightened in his seat. "Who is he?"

"Ronald, aka Ronnie Dahl." Garrett's gaze

locked on his. "Last known address is Chicago."

"Do you know him?" Liam asked.

Wyatt nodded, his mind spinning. He'd heard the name in conjunction with the Johnny Raffa organization. He hadn't recognized the face, but fingerprints didn't lie. He hadn't stopped to examine him more closely in the dark.

Either way, knowing one of the Raffa hit men had tried to kill Abby was sobering.

And now he firmly believed his boss was working with the Raffa criminal organization, too.

bsolutely." Wyatt's expression lightened. truly grateful."

arrett and Liam left to get the phones and keys to their replacement vehicle. Abby hed out to cover Wyatt's hand with hers. his worked out well. I'm glad we trusted m."

"Me, too. Too bad they don't have jurisction in Chicago." Wyatt turned so they re facing each other. "You've been amazg through this, Abby. I hope and pray we nd your father."

She nodded, trying not to become mesmerzed by his intense green gaze. She trusted Wyatt as a protector, but she knew better than o allow their relationship to turn personal. "We will." She needed to believe her father would show up at the burned farmhouse.

And if he didn't? She swallowed against he lump of fear lodged in her throat. She had no idea where to go next.

"How soon can we head back to Duncan Lane?" She held Wyatt's gaze.

"Not for at least twenty-four hours. I don't want to show up too quickly, since the bad uys found us not far from that location. Besides, I'd rather head to Chicago."

She winced, knowing he was right. "What's e plan?"

FIVE

Abby glanced between the three law enforcement men surrounding her. "I don't understand. Why would someone connected with Johnny Raffa come after me?"

"Because I highly suspect my boss is working for them." Wyatt's tone was hard and flat. "And he wants anyone he can't control who's connected to the Marchese case to be eliminated."

"Certainly seems that way," Liam agreed. "Although, to bc honest, all you have is theory and supposition."

"I know." Wyatt pinched the bridge of his nose. "That's the most difficult part of this mess. Finding someone to trust."

Wyatt's despair was troubling. Abby spoke reassuringly. "Hey, we'll figure it out."

He tried to smile, but it didn't reach his eyes. "We will. But my main objective is to keep you and your father safe."

Last night, his goal had been to get information from her father to bring his boss down. Now he'd realigned his mission a bit. She appreciated his determination to keep them safe, but she also knew that would never happen unless they were able to get to the bottom of this mess.

And soon. Before another Johnny Raffa hit man came after them.

"I've sent a deputy out to find the dead guy and the damaged sedan," Garrett said, breaking the silence. "Based on your description of the events, I think we can agree the shooting was in self-defense."

"It was," she felt compelled to speak up. "I saw the whole thing. Wyatt didn't have a choice but to kill him."

"I would have preferred to take him alive to find out who sent him and why," Wyatt agreed. "At least now we know that much. What about the black Ford truck with the license plate numbers of 5-6-2? Any hits on that?"

"I found a black Ford truck registered with those numbers, but it was reported stolen." Garrett shrugged. "We've sent the information to our deputies, but so far they haven't found the vehicle. I can let you know when we do."

"That would be great, although I don't have a replacement phone yet." The "
att's mouth kicked up. "I need "I a

"I can help with that." Liam r C
"I'll send someone out to buy a the
posable phones. That way, we'll rea
the numbers and keep in touch." "T

Abby was touched by the su the
Liam and Garrett. Rachel was ri
were good men. di

"Thank you." Wyatt met Liam's w
you have a car rental place in town ir
the SUV under my name, but might f
to rent me another one."

"No, sorry." Liam glanced at Garre
added, "But I can loan you a replace
hicle. We can get your leased SUV wi
repaired and hold it here until this is o

"I can pay you," Wyatt offered, but
waved a hand.

"It's no problem. We end up with a few
vehicles from time to time." He grinned
"Happy to donate one for a good cause

"You've been great, Liam, and G
too." Wyatt's tone was sincere. "I app
everything you've done for us."

"And they say Feds and local cop s
get along," Garrett joked. "We'll pro
wrong." th

"I need to think about how to get Larry Turks, the SAC, special agent in charge of the entire Chicago office, to believe me."

"What will prevent him from speaking directly to Hawthorne?" She couldn't hide her nervousness about this approach.

Wyatt gave her hand a squeeze, then stood and paced. "It's a good question. Especially since Hawthorne had likely told him I'm the bad guy. But I may have to try."

"Because?" She wasn't following his logic.

"Normally I would get SAC approval before approaching an attorney with an offer to exchange key information about a dirty cop with a lesser jail sentence." He shrugged. "Then again, it may be better to approach Gardner first, show him my creds and let him know I would be willing to get the SAC to agree to the terms, if his client is interested."

She nodded thoughtfully. "I like that better. If Franco and/or Tony are interested in cooperating, then you can go to the SAC with the proposal." It wasn't a bad idea. "If the big boss knows there's even a possibility of a dirty cop, he may just agree to the plan."

"Exactly." He stopped pacing and turned to face her. "I won't lie to Gardner. I can't promise anything up-front, so he may just toss us out on the street. But if I explain about the potential leak within the FBI and the Johnny Raffa hit man coming after us, the lawyer might listen. Especially if he understands his clients may be holding their silence to their own detriment." He spread his hands wide. "At the very least, he may go back and talk with them to find out more. It's worth a try."

"Are there risks?"

He grimaced. "Sure. If I'm wrong and there is no dirty cop, I've just given Gardner some appeal arguments. But I don't think I am. There's no other explanation for the danger dogging us."

"I agree." It felt good to have a solid plan. "Let's do it."

Another fifteen minutes passed before Liam returned with two cell phones and a set of car keys. The phones were already activated and powered up.

"I have both these numbers added to my personal phone," Liam said as he handed them each a small phone along with a bag containing the chargers. "You'll see my number is in your phones, too. I won't be able to help you in Chicago—I've had only limited interaction with the cops there—but if you run into trouble here in Green Lake County, let me know."

"We will. Thanks, Liam." Wyatt pocketed the phone, tucked the paperwork beneath his arm, then offered the sheriff his hand. "I owe you one."

"Nah, consider it a favor among professionals." Liam grinned. "Although once this is over, my wife, Shauna, and I wouldn't mind a steak dinner."

For the first time in what seemed like forever, Wyatt chuckled softly. "I'd love that. Count me in."

"Good. Come on, I'll show you the car." Liam held the door to the interview room open for them. "It's not pretty, has some rust on it, but the engine is in great shape and it will get you where you need to go."

Outside, the bright sun was already warming the chilly fall temps, reflecting off the yellow, orange and red leaves on the surrounding trees. As they crossed the parking lot, she saw a dark gray SUV that had several spots of rust along the edges of the wheel wells.

"This is perfect." Wyatt used the key fob to unlock the vehicle. He opened the door and set the bag of charging cords in the back seat along with the interview transcripts.

"Stay safe," Liam said, his expression turning serious.

"That's the plan." Wyatt waited for her to get in the passenger seat before sliding behind the wheel. Moments later, they were back on the road.

"Chicago, here we come," she said in a low voice.

"Yes." He glanced at her. "Keep trying to reach your father. I don't like that he's out there on his own."

"I will." She stared out the window for a moment, before adding, "I don't like it, either. But my dad has been running from the Marchese family for years, never getting caught. He is extremely good at staying off grid."

"So far off grid that we can't reach him," Wyatt said. "That's not helpful."

There was no denying he was right, but her father had likely been at the cabin in the woods, staying away because of Wyatt.

Or because he'd sensed danger from the Johnny Raffa hit man.

She lifted her gaze up toward the sky, praying her dad would stay safe.

And that they'd be able to reunite very soon.

The traffic wasn't too bad until they reached the border between Wisconsin and Illinois. Wyatt decided they should stop for lunch and fill up the gas tank. It had only been half-full when Liam had given it to them, and he would rather be prepared in case they came across another gunman.

He told himself there was no way for Hawthorne or any of Raffa's men to track them. No cell phone, no vehicle, and he would pay cash for everything from here on. Thankfully, he'd gotten plenty of cash before he'd taken his leave of absence from the Bureau.

There was no doubt he'd need every dollar to get through the next few days.

"This brings back memories," Abby said softly, as they crossed into Illinois.

"Bad ones?" He glanced at her.

"Some good, some bad. Especially the shooting attempt at Huntington Park."

He winced. "I didn't expect that to happen, Abby. I'm truly sorry about what you and your dad have suffered."

"I realize now that it wasn't your fault," she said quickly. "But at the time? Yeah, I must admit we were upset at being set up."

Her comment reminded him of the way she'd helped with having both Franco and Tony Marchese arrested. He wouldn't mind hearing more about what had happened from her, since he couldn't read the transcript while driving. "We'll stop at the family restaurant off the next exit. There's a gas station nearby."

"Okay. I'm ready to eat," she admitted.

After filling the tank, he parked outside the restaurant. The hour was a quarter to one in the afternoon, but thankfully the dining area wasn't too full. He requested a spot in the corner away from the other diners so they could speak freely without being overheard.

He waited until their server had taken their orders, before leaning forward. "How exactly did you help bring down Tony and Franco?"

She stared down at the table for a moment, then met his gaze. "After the shooting at Huntington Park, my dad and I split up. He wanted me to leave the area, but I decided to keep tabs on Franco, and followed him to Green Lake. It was then I realized they planned to use my twin sister to bring my dad out of hiding."

"You were very brave to head into danger like that."

She sighed. "Brave or stupid, it's hard to know for sure. The truth? I was tired of running. And I knew they wouldn't stop looking for us."

"No, they would not have stopped." The leak within the FBI was still searching for them. He frowned and added, "That reminds me—we need time to read through the transcript Liam gave us. It may help us approach his lawyer, Jerome Gardner."

"I can drive if you want to review them," she offered.

He arched a brow. "Are you sure? The traffic will only get worse from here."

"I've handled it before. And if there is something in those interviews that will help us, I'm all for you doing that."

"Okay, sounds good to me." Their server arrived with their meals, a burger for him and turkey wrap for Abby. He clasped his hands together and bowed his head.

"Will you pray out loud?" Abby whispered.

He couldn't help but smile. "Of course. Dear Lord, we thank You for this food we are about to eat. We ask that You continue to keep Abby and her father safe in Your care. Amen."

"And Wyatt, too. Amen." She met his gaze. "Thank you."

"We're going to get through this, Abby." He reached across the table to take her hand in his. "God will watch over us."

"We attended church when I was young, but lately?" She winced. "I think my dad must have given up on his beliefs."

"I'm sorry to hear that, because we need our Lord the most during difficult times." He offered a reassuring smile. "It's not always easy to understand why some of us are sent along a harder path than others, but we must have faith that God is watching over us."

"I'll try." She stared at their joined hands for a moment before tugging hers away to pick up her turkey wrap.

They ate in silence for several minutes. "Do you have any idea what your father planned to tell me at the meeting that never happened?"

She chewed for a moment, then took a sip of water. "He gave you the business information, first, right?"

"Yes. And that was very helpful. We were able to bring in several low-level crooks involved in illegal arms dealing, but they either refused to cooperate or didn't know anything about Tony, Franco or Walter."

She nodded thoughtfully. "Dad told me he didn't want to give you everything he knew in one sitting. I think he was hoping he wouldn't have to keep coming back, that you'd get enough on the Marchese men without his giving you more."

"Why was that?" He asked.

She met his gaze. "Because he didn't really want to testify against them in court. He knew that would put me and Rachel in danger."

"The Marcheses went after you both, anyway," he said.

"Yes, but that was probably because of the FBI leak. We were easy to find." She leaned forward. "Sure, me and my dad could go off grid again, but Rachel was the most vulnerable. He knew she would not leave the Amish community."

It was a good point. "Okay, I get it. But it would be helpful to know what he was planning to tell me during our second meeting."

"It probably doesn't matter now that they're both in jail, but I'm sure he was planning to tell you about the connections they had with the local police, and about the murder he was supposed to carry out."

The dirty cops weren't a surprise, but murder? "Who was involved in the murder?"

"Tony gave the order, but Franco took my dad along to do the deed. When my dad refused, Franco took the guy out then said it was my dad's turn to kill the next guy to prove his loyalty to the family. My dad was only eighteen at the time, and that was when he decided to cut all ties with his family and to run."

"That sounds horrible," he admitted. "I don't blame him for doing that."

"I think he liked the simple life of the Amish, their faith in God, and the way they avoided all technology. And he truly loved my mother, too. He told me he was blessed to have had seven years with the Amish. But Walter and Tony didn't rest until they'd found him."

"Probably because there is no statute of limitations on murder. And your father's testimony would have put both Tony and Franco in jail for murder and for their illegal arms dealing, along with whatever other criminal acts they'd done."

"Where they are now," she agreed. "I'm more concerned about Johnny Raffa's hit man coming after us."

"Yeah, me, too." He still thought he could use the Raffa family taking over the Marchese businesses to his advantage when it was time to chat with Gardner.

Anxious to get back on the road, they quickly finished eating. He paid in cash, then led the way out to the borrowed SUV. After giving Abby the keys, he grabbed the paperwork from the back, along with the bag of phone cords.

Abby backed out of their parking space and headed to the interstate. Peeking inside the bag, he was shocked to realize Liam had tucked a wad of cash inside.

He held it out for Abby to see. "I owe Liam and his wife more than a steak dinner."

"For sure." She smiled. "I guess I was wrong to be so leery of Liam and Garrett."

After what she and her father had suffered, he didn't blame her for avoiding the police.

Wyatt used his new phone to call the law offices of Gardner and Twain. The woman who answered the phone agreed to connect him to Jerome Gardner. Unfortunately, the guy didn't answer, forcing him to leave a message.

"I would like to set up a meeting to discuss a matter that will be of interest to you and your clients Franco and Tony. Please call me back at this number." He rattled it off. "Thank you."

"You didn't leave your name," Abby pointed out. "Or mention their last name."

"No, and I didn't really want to mention Tony and Franco, either, but I'm sure he wouldn't bother to call me back unless I gave him something." He tapped the phone in the palm of his hand. "I hope he is intrigued enough to return my call."

"I'm sure he will." Abby's gaze remained focused on the traffic, which was growing worse by the minute. "We're about forty-five minutes from the Dettmer office building. Maybe we'll have better luck in person."

"I hope so." He turned his attention to the

transcript Liam had provided. He wasn't surprised that Franco had put the blame for everything on his cousin Tony's shoulders. There was no doubt that Tony had taken over as the leader of the organized crime ring once his father had been diagnosed with Alzheimer's disease.

Unfortunately, there was not a single mention of anyone helping them from within the FBI or even specific names of local law enforcement. He wondered if that was simply because Franco wasn't aware of Hawthorne helping them, or if that was a bargaining chip he and Tony were waiting to use when they were further along in the process. They had been arrested in May, and the wheels of justice turned slowly.

He made a mental note of the businesses Franco had admitted to being used as a funnel for dirty money. That information could be helpful in the future.

When he finished, he was relieved to see they were close to Chicago's downtown area. "Let's find a parking garage. It will be easier to walk the rest of the way."

"There used to be one—oh, there it is." She shot a glance over her shoulder and nosed the SUV into the narrow opening between two cars. He couldn't help but grin. Chicago driv-

go," Wyatt said in a low voice.

we need to stay and provide state-
More cops had arrived, along with
mbulances. She belatedly realized
re others who'd been hurt, too.

was about to shake his head, when
cers strode toward them. "You both

we were able to take cover." Wyatt
d. "I didn't see anything, though. Two
s rang out the moment we were head-
the building."

o were you planning to see?" one of-
ked.

held back, not sure how much Wyatt
d to say. "I was looking for a good
heard there was a law office in here."
kfully, the cop simply nodded without
anything more. "I'll need your names
record."

yne Greer and this is Amelia Minow,"
said without hesitation.

schooled her features to hide her sur-
The cop wrote them down, then was
ask for their ID's when he was inter-
by another witness.

tt took her hand and tugged her away
he scene, heading in the direction
just come from. They had to elbow

ers were known to be aggressive and Abby
was no exception.

Parking fees were high, too, but there was
no way around it. The biggest problem was
that the machines only accepted credit cards.
Something he had no intention of using. He
offered the driver behind him extra cash
along with the full-day fee, if he'd pay for
the both of them.

The stranger readily agreed.

Ten minutes later they were back on the
street level, making their way down Michigan
Avenue. The weather was nice enough that
there were plenty of pedestrians around, too,
which helped them to mesh with the crowd.

Another fifteen minutes later they finally
reached the tall building. Near the front door,
he hesitated, trying to formulate a plan in his
head, when he heard a shout.

"Gun!" A split second later, a gunshot
echoed loudly. He instinctively ducked, pulling Abby down near a concrete planter, so he
could cover her with his body.

How had they been found so quickly?
From his call to Jerome's office? As people
screamed and began running, he knew they
needed to move, before the gunman could
take aim and fire again.

SIX

In all her years of hiding from the mob, she hadn't been shot at as much as she had these past twenty-four hours. It was difficult to see who was shooting at her now, between the concrete planter she was crouched behind and the way Wyatt covered her.

The gunfire stopped, but the screams of pedestrians and the wail of sirens echoed loudly around them. Had the shooter left the scene?

"Stay down." Wyatt stood upright, raking his gaze over the area.

She peeked over the rim of the planter, gasping when she saw a man lying on the ground. He didn't move. Even from here, she could see the blood pooling beneath him.

"Was the shooter aiming at us? Or that guy?" she asked in a whisper.

Wyatt frowned. "Probably us. The other guy must have gotten in the way."

She felt sick knowing this man had taken

the bullet meant for
wrong, on so many l

But she hadn't ask
dad had tried to do th

Squad cars pulled u
ing, several officers
emerging from the veh
to search for the shoot

This was the kind o
pened in movies. Abb
was living it now.

More cops arrived, e
didn't move from the pl
out his hand. "You ca
now."

No, they weren't saf
she understood what he
had taken off. Only a foo
after hearing police si
hand, she allowed him
her knees shaking with
adrenaline rush.

Two officers crouche
the ground. They shook
of them covered the gu

The stranger who'd t
for them was dead. N
belly, the turkey wrap
back up. She swallowe

"Let's
"Don
ments?"
several
there w

Wya
two off
okay?"

"Yes
grimac
gunsho
ing int

"Wh
ficer a

Abb
planne
lawyer

Tha
asking
for the

"Wa
Wyatt

Abb
prise.
about t
rupted

Wya
from t
they'd

past a group of gawkers located beyond the circle of police vehicles.

No one stopped them, and it was only when they were far enough away that Wyatt turned into the closest coffee shop.

"Shouldn't we head to the car?" She couldn't help glancing over her shoulder. "What if the shooter comes back?"

"I'm sure he's long gone, and I don't want to get the car yet." He steered her toward a table in the corner. "Coffee?"

Her fingers were still trembling, so she shook her head. "I'm shaky enough, thanks."

"I know, but we need to come up with another plan to meet with Jerome Gardner. We need to make a purchase to hang out here for a while."

"Fine, I'll have a decaf coffee." Normally she didn't bother with decaf, but nothing about this morning had been normal. Not the gunfire between the burned farmhouse and Green Lake or this recent attempt to kill them.

She sank into a seat while Wyatt ordered their drinks. It was impossible to wipe the image of the dead man from her mind. She didn't know him and hadn't been the one to pull the trigger, yet she felt guilty anyway.

Wyatt returned with their order, taking the

chair closest to her. "I'm sorry you had to go through that."

She removed the cover to her coffee and took a tentative sip. "Not your fault, but I'm not sure why we're staying here. The phone call you made to Gardner's office must have caused this."

"Yeah. I can't think of another way for Hawthorne or anyone else to have tracked us here," he agreed. "But that means Gardner's phone is bugged."

"Bugged?" She stared at him in shock. "By the FBI?"

"Who else?" He scowled over his coffee. "This has the Feds written all over it."

"Don't they need a warrant?"

"Yeah, if the tap was legal. I'm thinking it wasn't going to be used by anyone but Hawthorne himself."

She stared at him. "Then why are we sticking around?"

"Because they sent the gunman to stop us, which makes me think we're on the right track." He reached over to grasp her hand. "I know I'm asking a lot, but please trust me. We really need to speak with Gardner."

"I trust you, Wyatt, but the cops are going to be staked out at the building all day."

"Yeah, I know." He sipped his coffee, still

holding on to her hand. "I'm sure he's hunkered down in the office, too. What we really need is to speak to him in person."

She clung to his hand, secretly needing the physical connection. Odd how quickly she and Wyatt had become a team. It was a partnership she hadn't wanted, especially after her friend Greg Sharma had been killed helping her. She'd been determined to remain independent moving forward.

Now, she couldn't imagine doing any of this without Wyatt.

"He'll need to leave the building eventually," Wyatt said. "Probably near five o'clock."

"We're going to hang out here for three hours?" She tried to hide her dismay. "That's a long time."

"We'll move to another location, soon." He released her hand and pulled out his disposable phone. "I'm not sure if the Feds can track this number as I used it to make the call." He sighed, then shut the device down, stomped on it and tossed it in the trash. "Let me borrow your phone. I'll call the office again. Maybe the same receptionist will answer."

"Sure." She pushed the device toward him, then wrapped her fingers around the cup as he made the call. Less than a minute later, he sighed and lowered the device. "No answer and I'm not leaving another message."

"The office must be in chaos after the shooting. For all we know, Gardner and the other occupants of the building have been sent home."

"You're right. They easily could have shut the place down." He looked so dejected she felt bad for bringing it up. "We'll head back that way in an hour, see how things are going. If we learn the place has been shut down, then we'll find someplace to stay for the night."

"Hotels in this area will be pricey and unlikely to take cash."

"That's where having a car comes in handy." His smile was crooked. "We'll find something well outside of Chicago city limits. And we'll pick up another set of disposable phones just to be on the safe side, too."

"Can't wait." She'd tried to keep her tone light, but the seriousness of their situation made it difficult. A man had died today.

And it was only a matter of time before the gunman came after them, again.

Wyatt hated to admit he'd run out of ideas. His entire plan had been centered on getting information from Gardner. Without that intel he wasn't sure what to do next. He could go through the transcripts again, but so far they hadn't been very helpful.

"We might want to get that room sooner than later," Abby said. "Watching the news may help fill the gaps."

Television! He quickly stood. "You're brilliant, Abby. There's a sports pub nearby that has televisions mounted all over the place."

"Far from brilliant." She flushed and tossed her empty coffee cup in the trash. "Just logical."

It occurred to him he didn't know much about her other than the fact she and her dad had been hiding from the Marchese family for years. He was curious to know more, yet it didn't feel right to ask if she'd graduated high school or attended college.

He was afraid the answers to both questions might be no, which saddened him. She was bright and deserved opportunity.

Outside, he made sure to keep Abby to his right, so that he was between her and the road. Hopefully, the gunman would assume they'd leave the area, and normally that would have been his first choice.

But they needed something to go on. He couldn't accept the idea of failing to bring Hawthorne to justice.

The sports-themed pub was almost a

mile away. As they entered the building, he glanced at the various televisions, searching for one that wasn't showing games.

"Table for two?" a hostess asked.

"Yes, in that booth over there, please." He gestured to the one not far from a television that was displaying the news.

"Follow me." She escorted them to the table, then set menus down. "Sasha will be your server today."

He heard Abby groan under her breath at the idea of more food, and fought a smile. "Great, thanks."

"I'm stuffed," she said when they were alone. "You might have the appetite of an ox, but I can't possibly eat anything more."

"We'll get an appetizer." He gestured toward the live news coverage of the shooting. The news program offered closed-caption capabilities as there would be no way for them to hear this television over the others. "It's worth it to get the information we need."

"I guess." She did not look enthused as Sasha came and took their order for soft drinks and nachos.

They fell silent as they read the closed-caption recording of the news. It wasn't perfect—sometimes there were words or phrases that didn't make any sense—but Police Chief

Rex Jericho was clearly stating his men would continue searching for any information on the identity of the gunman.

"Maybe we should send a tip to the hotline to look at anyone with connections to Johnny Raffa," Abby said. "I'm sure this guy is hired muscle for him, too."

It was a logical assumption, and while it was tempting to make the call, he shook his head. "We can't. There's no way to know for sure Raffa's hit man is involved. My boss could have found hired muscle somewhere else. Besides, the police would want to follow up with us, and we can't risk doing that, yet."

She looked disappointed but didn't say anything more. When their nachos arrived, he reached across the table and took her hand.

"Dear Lord, we thank You for protecting us earlier today and ask that You please provide us courage and guidance as we seek the truth. Comfort the families of those injured and killed. Amen."

"Amen," Abby echoed.

He wasn't necessarily hungry, either, but took a bite of the nacho chips anyway. Hoping this wasn't a waste of time, he continued watching the news.

"Wyatt?" Abby's voice drew his attention

from the television. So far, he hadn't learned anything he hadn't already known.

"What?" He frowned. "Is something wrong?"

"Two cops just walked in and they're just standing in the doorway, looking around." Her voice dropped lower. "Do you think they're searching for us?"

He saw them now, and a shiver darted down his spine. It was difficult not to be paranoid, especially knowing the Marchese and likely the Raffa family had connections within law enforcement. Still, he couldn't imagine how they'd been followed to the coffee shop and now here. He glanced toward the restrooms, which weren't too far away.

Should they stay here, hoping they weren't the focus of the officers' attention? Or try to escape?

At that moment the policemen turned to look in the opposite direction. Wyatt pulled cash from his pocket, dropped it on the table and stood. "Come with me."

To her credit, Abby jumped up to join him. They moved swiftly toward the restrooms. Once they were out of view from the dining room, he looked for a way out.

"This way," Abby said, tugging on his hand. Remembering how she'd mentioned working as a server and a cook to earn money, he allowed her to take the lead. She headed to a short hallway that, from the sounds of banging pots and pans, he knew led to the kitchen.

Several pairs of eyes glanced at them as Abby wove through the crowded space.

"Hey, you can't be in here," someone called out.

Abby ignored the voice, relentlessly moving through the room. Trusting her instincts, he followed close behind.

A moment later, she burst out of a back door leading to a grimy area behind the building. Without stopping, she skirted the dumpster and headed for the street.

"Good move," he said with admiration.

She flashed a smile. "Kitchens always have a back exit. It wouldn't look good to carry garbage through the dining room where the customers can see and smell it."

"True." He stepped around her so he was positioned closest to the road. She moved closer in a way that made him want to put his arm around her. He managed to stick with simply holding her hand. "Those cops may not have been looking for us," he pointed out. "We may have left a perfectly good plate of nachos behind for no reason."

"I'm sorry, but I had a bad feeling about the officers." She sighed and shook her head.

"It's hard to say if my instincts were on target, or my nerves are shot from everything we've been through."

"Doesn't matter. It's better to err on the side of caution. Especially since we always suspected the Marchese and now the Raffa family, had cops on their payroll." He shot her a look of admiration. "I would trust your instincts any time, Abby."

"Thanks." Her cheeks went pink and he was fascinated by the way a simple compliment made her blush. Abby was tough on the outside, tossing a log at him and escaping through the window, but he suspected she was a marshmallow on the inside. She cleared her throat and asked, "Do you think they figured out we didn't give our real names?"

"I doubt they've had time to run all the witnesses' names through the system." He hadn't liked lying to the officers but having his real name on their list wasn't an option. That would have made it far too easy for Hawthorne to track him down. He'd sent up a silent prayer that God might forgive him. "But if the shooter knew he missed us, he may have reported that failure to his boss."

"And that boss may have asked his officers to find us," she said, finishing his thought.

"Yeah." He paused at a stoplight, waiting

for the traffic signal to change so they could cross the street. "Okay, since going back to Gardner's office isn't an option, we'll head back to pick up the SUV. The better plan is to try and get in touch with him first thing tomorrow morning."

"Sounds good," Abby agreed.

They had to go several blocks out of their way to circle around to the parking structure where they'd left the borrowed SUV.

By the time they retrieved their car and stopped to purchase another disposable phone, it was close to five o'clock. He found a cheap motel and was relieved the clerk had agreed to provide two adjoining rooms for cash. Granted, his flashing his FBI creds helped.

The rooms were nothing special, but they were clean. When he'd stopped to get the phone, he'd picked up some toiletries, too. He brought the bag in for Abby just as she was turning on the television.

"I wish they'd tell us the identity of the man who died." Her brow furrowed as she perched on the bottom edge of the bed. "I can't help feeling guilty about how he was hit when it should have been one of us."

"We didn't pull the trigger," he reminded her gently. He set the toothbrush, toothpaste and hairbrush on the table. "And they won't tell us until his family has been notified."

She winced. "His poor family."

"I know." He understood her empathy for the situation and found himself hoping and praying her father was still alive, too. He activated and charged his new phone while Abby watched the news.

"I hope they don't mention they're looking for us," she murmured. "The hotel manager would probably turn us over to the cops without blinking an eye."

"I doubt Hawthorne wants my name splashed on the news just yet," he said dryly. At least, he hoped not. He'd assumed his boss's goal would be to kill him, then splash his name on the news identifying him as a traitor.

He fell silent, dropping down beside Abby as the commercial ended and the TV news anchor appeared back on the screen. A large red breaking news banner flashed over her head.

"This is Tracy Andrews reporting live from downtown Chicago, where a gunman opened fire, killing one man and wounding several others." The camera panned from the serious-faced anchor to the tall building he and Abby had been about to enter hours earlier. "The police have just released the identity of the victim, who apparently works within the building."

The anchorwoman paused for dramatic effect before continuing. "The victim of the shooting is fifty-six-year-old Jerome Gardner, the managing partner of Gardner and Twain, LLC. That office is located on the sixth floor of the Dettmer office building you see here." Once again, the camera panned to the skyscraper behind her. "The police do not have a motive for this brutal slaying in broad daylight. However we have learned that Gardner and Twain are criminal defense attorneys, so this may be a case of a dissatisfied client extracting revenge."

Wyatt stopped listening, as the realization hit hard. The dead guy was Franco and Tony's lawyer.

Had Gardner been the real target all along? Or had he and Abby been the intended victims and the shooter had taken Gardner out by mistake?

Maybe. Yet speaking to Gardner was clearly no longer an option.

Which was exactly what the shooter had intended.

SEVEN

"This is not good," Abby whispered, her gaze glued to the television screen.

"No, it's not," Wyatt agreed. He jammed his fingers through his hair. "Hawthorne must be getting desperate, to take out a lawyer."

She frowned, glancing up at him. "I thought the bullets were meant for us?"

"Maybe the shooter figured he could take Gardner and us out at the same time."

"That's a huge coincidence," she argued. "Even if they had bugged Gardner's phone to learn we wanted to meet with him, they'd have no way of knowing when we'd show up."

"That much is true, but shooting a lawyer? That's a big deal. The cops will put every effort into finding the man responsible."

"But if the shooter is caught, the cops could easily make it look like a disgruntled client of Gardner and Twain. That would wrap up the case in a neat little bow."

"Exactly my thought. And getting rid of the lawyer curtails our strategy of waving a potential deal in front of his face. Starting over with a new attorney will stall us at the very least."

"So now what?" She turned a bit to look in his eyes, battling a wave of helplessness. "How long will it take for another lawyer to be assigned to Franco and Tony?"

"I'm hoping Kevin Twain will take over Gardner's case," he admitted. "Why wouldn't they keep their clients in-house?"

He made a good point. "Then we should talk to Twain."

"We can try." He grimaced. "First thing tomorrow morning, we'll head back to the law office. See if we can't convince Twain to meet with us. But I'm not going to call ahead this time."

"Yeah, that didn't work out so well." She scowled. "But wouldn't your boss figure out that Twain would take over the Marchese case? What was the point of killing Gardner, then?"

"I'm not sure." He looked so dejected she wanted to hug him. "It could be that there isn't much money left to continue representing the Marcheses. Especially if Raffa took over most of their illegal business ventures."

That possibility hadn't occurred to her, but she could easily imagine Twain washing his hands of Tony and Franco Marchese.

Money. Everything seemed to circle back to money.

"I guess we need to ask." She shrugged. "All he can do is to say no."

"True." Wyatt blew out a breath. "We need to find your dad. He must know something that can help us. Otherwise why would my boss be trying to find him?"

She'd done her best not to dwell on the danger her father was in, but his comment and their recent near misses caused her earlier fears to come rushing back in full force. "I don't know. The way his phone call cut off so abruptly seems to indicate he'd been found."

Wyatt's gaze mirrored her concern. "He's smart, Abby. If he was the one staying in the cabin, he's not being held by the bad guys any longer."

"I hope you're right." She tried to smile, but the nagging feeling of something being wrong wouldn't leave her alone. If her father was truly out of danger, he'd get a new disposable phone and call her.

Wouldn't he?

"We'll head back to Wisconsin after we stop by the law office tomorrow morning."

She nodded. His plan was reasonable. Too bad, she didn't feel very rational.

"Hey, let's try to remain positive." Wyatt wrapped his arm around her shoulders. "We're alive, Abby. The bad guys haven't beaten us yet. We have God on our side."

"Do we?" She desperately wanted to believe he was right about that. But while she'd joined him in prayer, deep down, she couldn't help wondering why her life had turned out this way.

Her dad had tried to do the right thing. He'd escaped from a life of crime. Embraced the Amish, joining their faith and becoming a family man.

His dream hadn't lasted long, and the past eighteen years they'd moved every year or two just to remain hidden from the Marcheses. But the stubborn mafia men had continued searching for them.

So her dad had decided to do the next right thing, provide information to the Feds.

Only to almost be shot at for his efforts.

Tears pricked her eyes. She wasn't a crier, so she quickly brushed them away.

"Abby, please." Wyatt sighed and pulled her closer still and pressed a kiss to her temple. "Try not to assume the worst."

She rested her head against his chest, drawing in his unique musky scent. If anyone had told her she'd be seeking comfort and strength from Wyatt Kane, she'd have laughed her head off.

Now she wished she could stay cradled in his arms forever.

Whoa, not forever. Where had that come from? She forced herself to ease away from him, keeping her gaze averted from his, lest he read her thoughts. "I—uh, should wash up."

He didn't move, his arm still wrapped around her shoulders. When she finally looked up at him, she found his green eyes mesmerizing. Then they dropped to her mouth.

Without thinking, she leaned in to kiss him. The moment their lips brushed, she realized this was a mistake.

Because kissing him knocked all rational thought from her mind, making her long for something she'd never dared wish for.

The warning lights flashing in the back of her mind finally gave her the strength to pull out of his warm embrace. "I—uh, sorry." She jumped off the edge of the bed. "Excuse me."

"Abby, I'm sorry…"

"No! Don't be." The last thing she wanted was for him to apologize for her kiss. Her cheeks heated with embarrassment. "I'm the one who should apologize. It's been a long day."

He didn't say anything, but the way he continued to hold her gaze made her knees feel weak. To stop from making an even bigger fool of herself, she swept the bag of toiletries off the table and headed to the tiny bathroom, closing the door firmly behind her.

Bracing her hands on the edge of the sink, she pulled herself together. But when she looked up, she wanted to groan. The mirror confirmed her fair skin had betrayed her. Her face was bright red.

Enough. This odd attraction she had for the man she'd once despised was not real. Their situation was abnormal, to say the least. Once the danger was over, she wouldn't see Wyatt again. He'd go back to his life with the FBI, while she and her dad would settle someplace, maybe even in Green Lake to be near Rachel.

Yes, that was a good plan for her future. One that didn't feature Wyatt at all.

Her stern lecture to her image helped calm her racing heart. After she finished using the facilities, she found the courage to face Wyatt.

He was waiting for her, still watching the news. "Hey, are you hungry?"

She wondered if he was always so focused on food. Remembering the nachos they'd barely touched, she took pity on him and nodded. "I could eat."

"Great. They offer pizza deliveries here." He paused, then asked, "You do like pizza, right?"

"Yes, I like pizza." She appreciated the way he'd lightened the tone. "But no anchovies."

"And no pineapple," he said. "Fruit does not belong on pizza."

She had to laugh. "Not my favorite, either."

"Great, I'll put the order in now." He stood and headed over to where he had his new disposable phone charging up. She was glad their relationship was back on a normal footing.

Even if she secretly longed for more.

That amazing kiss had changed everything. Wyatt tried to push the memory aside by ordering dinner, but it hadn't worked.

He still wanted to kiss her, again.

This was hardly the time or the place to think about Abby as an attractive woman. They were in grave danger, and he needed to put all his energy into bringing Hawthorne to justice.

Keeping his attention on the job hadn't

been a problem before. Hadn't Emma left him because of his dedication to his career? Back then he'd found it easy to forget about her as he worked.

Why couldn't he do that with Abby?

When they'd finished eating, he escaped to his room. He wanted to believe they were safe here for the night, but that didn't mean he was going to lower his guard.

Wyatt woke up every few hours, listening intently and peering through the window to search for potential threats before going back to sleep. He estimated he'd only gotten about five hours of sleep total, but that was better than nothing.

He wished he dared to call Kevin Twain directly, but the shooting incident made him leery of making the same mistake. He couldn't even say for sure the office would be open for business after Jerome Gardner's murder.

Should they go north to Wisconsin, instead? No, they needed to try to see Twain. They'd come this far. He couldn't just leave without attempting to find something to go on.

Hawthorne would not get away with this.

Abby was still sleeping, so he quickly showered, then turned his attention to breakfast. He thought it would be better to eat somewhere close to their destination.

What he really needed was a computer now that he didn't have his smartphone. He remembered seeing one in the hotel lobby, so he left Abby a note and headed down to use the device.

When he searched for the law office of Gardner and Twain, the first hit was related to the shooting incident. He scanned the article but didn't learn anything new. Pulling up the website, he navigated the pages until he found pictures of both Jerome Gardner and Kevin Twain.

Jerome looked to be the younger of the two men, or maybe Kevin just appeared older because he was bald. The website listed the address as being in the Dettmer Building, suite 6000.

He did a broader search on the Dettmer building itself, using a map program to get a three-sixty-degree view of the place. No way was he going to use the front door this time. He identified each of the other building entrances and exits. There were several to choose from, but one located on the southeast side seemed to offer the safest approach.

Lastly, he found a restaurant that offered parking located a mile from the Dettmer office building. They could eat and head over to see Twain. They wouldn't be gone long enough to risk their vehicle being booted or towed.

Satisfied with the plan, he rose. As he turned, he saw Abby walking toward him. It took every bit of willpower he possessed not to kiss her.

"Good morning." His smile faded when he caught the glint of anger in her eyes. "What? I left a note!"

"One I didn't see right away." She blew out a breath. "I was scared something had happened to you."

"I needed to borrow the computer." He felt guilty for worrying her. "I looked up the office building and found a restaurant close by. I figure we can eat there, then walk over in time to meet with Twain since they don't open until nine o'clock."

Her anger faded. "Okay. But next time? Wake me up rather than sneaking off."

"I will." He was surprised at how easily she gave up the argument, something Emma would never have done, as they turned back toward their rooms.

After Abby finished cleaning up, they headed out to the borrowed SUV. With the map in his mind, he had no trouble finding the restaurant.

Once they'd placed their order and had cups of coffee, he quickly told her about the side entrance he planned to use to get inside.

"There was nothing on the website about the office being closed for the day?"

"Nope." He didn't have anything against lawyers, but in his experience, they treated time as money. It would take something more drastic than an unexpected death to close, even for a few days. But then again, he tended to be cynical when it came to defense lawyers, especially those who chose to defend mafia bosses. "I guess we'll find out soon enough."

They were on their second cup of coffee before their meals arrived. Abby's teasing about his large appetite had stung a bit, but he knew that it was better to eat when you had the chance. If they ended up dodging more gunfire there wouldn't be time.

Abby didn't reach for her silverware, obviously waiting for him to pray. He took her hand and bowed his head. "Lord, we offer our thanks for the meal You've provided for us. We ask for Your continued strength and courage as we seek to bring criminals to justice. In Jesus's name, amen."

"And please keep my father safe in Your care, too. Amen," Abby said.

"I should have included your father. Thanks for adding him. I'm sure we'll find him very soon." He gently squeezed her hand before releasing it.

"I hope so." Her smile didn't reach her eyes, but at least she wasn't crying. Last night, her tears had ripped a hole in his heart.

If he could go back and do things over again, he wouldn't have tracked Abby in hopes of finding her father. He couldn't deny that he'd brought this danger upon them.

All the more reason to dedicate himself to keeping them safe now. Unfortunately, the only way they'd ever be safe was by finding proof of Hawthorne's guilt.

A vicious circle, he silently admitted.

"What's wrong?" Abby frowned. "You look upset."

"Not upset, frustrated." He shrugged and took a bite of his omelet, which the server had just delivered. "If this doesn't work…"

"If anyone can convince Twain to cooperate, it's you, Wyatt." She offered a lopsided smile. "You managed to get me over on your side, remember?"

"Yeah and brought danger with me." He couldn't hide his self-disgust. "Maybe if I had gone over Hawthorne's head instead of heading out to look for you and your father, you'd both be safe by now."

"That's not true. I lost contact with my father before you arrived on the scene. I think he must have been found by one of the gunmen." She toyed with her eggs, then met his gaze. "Let's be honest, Wyatt. If your boss considers me and my dad as loose ends, he'll keep sending thugs until we're no longer a threat."

He nodded slowly. "You're right. And you can add me to that list, too. In fact, Hawthorne might consider me a larger threat, mostly because he knows I can try to convince the higher-ups about his culpability in all of this."

"There, you see? None of this is your fault."

"You're being nicer than I deserve." His appetite had vanished, but he forced himself to keep eating. "Thank you."

"Hey, we're a team, remember?" She managed a reassuring smile. "We're in this together."

The way she'd turned his words back on him made him smile. Yet in that moment, he made a promise that once they'd found her father, he'd find a safe place to put them both while he went on alone to bring his boss down.

He couldn't stand the idea of having any

more blood on his hands. Not that he was directly responsible for Jerome Gardner's death, but he'd certainly played an unwitting role in the poor guy's murder.

And he would not let anything happen to Abby and Peter Miller, either.

They lingered over their meal until eight thirty. They wouldn't need the entire thirty minutes to get to the Dettmer office building, but he wanted to be early.

After he'd paid for their meals, they headed outside. He took Abby's hand, mostly because he wanted to.

But when she shot him a curious look, he said, "It's best if we appear to be a casual couple out for a stroll."

"A romantic walk through the city at eight thirty in the morning?" She arched one brow. "Not sure that's going to fly."

"It will if we act like tourists, checking out the big city for the first time."

She laughed softly, while continuing to hold his hand. "Okay, I'm in."

Despite his intent to look like tourists, he set a brisk pace while constantly sweeping his gaze over the other pedestrians around them. Being out in the open after several shooting attempts made him feel vulnerable.

It seemed like most of the foot traffic at

this hour of the morning were people walking to work. Those who were dressed casually headed toward restaurants or stores, while those in business suits were no doubt en route to one of the many office buildings. Dozens streamed from various subway stops. He was familiar with them, as he'd commuted to the FBI offices using the subway, too.

Subways had cameras, though, so he planned to avoid them. The crowds bothered him and he couldn't help comparing the massive amount of people here to the quiet town of Green Lake. He knew the sheriff had experienced more than his share of crime, but Wyatt had to assume that Liam and Garrett preferred the rural life compared to that of a large metropolitan area.

As they grew closer to the Dettmer office building, he slowed his pace, searching for anyone who seemed suspicious. There was no sign of the police cars that had been there the day before, although they did pass a couple of squads on their walk.

"This area doesn't look familiar," Abby said in a low voice.

"Because we're approaching the building from the opposite direction from yesterday." They waited to cross the street. "See the building two blocks ahead? That's our destination."

"I see it." She tightened her grip on his hand.

They reached the skyscraper a few minutes before nine. Wyatt noticed there weren't nearly as many people going inside the building using this side entrance, which was exactly what he'd hoped for.

His gaze landed on a man wearing a hooded sweatshirt, hanging near the corner. He abruptly changed directions, taking Abby to the next block.

"I saw him, too," she whispered. "Is he a hired gun?"

"I'm not sure. Let's circle the next block, then head back. If he's still there, we'll know he's waiting for someone." Like the two of them, he thought grimly.

"Okay."

He made sure to take a full fifteen minutes before approaching the Dettmer building. When they paused at the traffic light, he saw the hooded guy. His back was turned and he was walking away.

"Hurry," he whispered. When the light changed, he and Abby sprinted across the street and went straight to the side door. He opened it and they quickly disappeared inside. He pulled the door closed, then took Abby's hand again as they approached the elevator.

"What if he's still out there when it's time to leave?" Abby asked breathlessly.

"We'll find a different way out." He stabbed the elevator button, shooting a quick glance over his shoulder. They were risking a lot by being here.

He silently prayed this trip would be worth the effort. And that the hooded man wasn't waiting for them with a gun when they were finished.

EIGHT

Doing her best not to show her apprehension, Abby stood calmly beside Wyatt as they took the elevator to the sixth floor. Their reflection in the shiny elevator door made her realize they were not appropriately attired for a meeting with an attorney.

In his flannel shirt, leather jacket and scuffed jeans, Wyatt wasn't dressed as a federal agent, which would likely raise a red flag with Kevin Twain. Her dark coat covering a sweatshirt and jeans wasn't any better. Still, all they needed was five minutes to confirm Twain was interested in a possible deal.

Then it would be up to Wyatt to find someone within the Chicago FBI office he could trust, to make that happen.

The elevator opened, revealing a plush office lobby that was clearly visible behind wide glass doors. The logo of Gardner and Twain was mounted above the receptionist's head.

Her stomach knotted, knowing Gardner was no longer with the firm.

Wyatt paused for a moment, looking up and down the hallway before opening the glass door. The receptionist frowned when they walked in, but she politely asked, "May I help you?"

She hung back, letting Wyatt take the lead. He pulled out his FBI badge and held it up. "I'm Agent Kane. Please forgive my attire, I'm working undercover. I'd like to speak briefly with Attorney Twain. It's important."

The receptionist considered his badge, but then shook her head. "I'm sorry, but you must have an appointment to speak with our attorneys."

Wyatt leaned forward. "It's critical I speak with him about Attorney Gardner's clients, Tony and Franco Marchese. I'm concerned Gardner's death was related to them."

Now the woman's eyes widened. She waved a hand indicating they should step back, before reaching for the phone.

Abby couldn't hear what the receptionist said. The conversation was brief. When she replaced the receiver in its cradle, she looked up at them. "Attorney Twain will be with you shortly."

"Thank you." Wyatt's smile didn't seem

to soften the woman one iota. Instead she scowled, as if she hadn't wanted Wyatt and Abby to be granted an unscheduled meeting with Twain. Maybe they were putting a wrench in the woman's tight schedule.

Regardless, Abby was thrilled they'd gotten this far. She and Wyatt sat together on a leather sofa that was nicer than anything she'd ever owned in her entire life.

Being a criminal defense attorney must pay well.

Attorney Kevin Twain didn't make them wait long. A minute later, a grim bald man who appeared to be in his sixties approached. He didn't try to hide his annoyance at the way they'd shown up without an appointment.

"Yes." Wyatt stood. "And this is my colleague, Abby. We appreciate you giving us a moment of your time."

"Five minutes," was his curt response. "My office is this way."

They followed him down a hallway, passing several other offices along the way. Associates, no doubt.

Twain gestured to the two chairs in front of his desk. He sat, facing them. "What's this about Gardner's death being related to his clients?"

"I have reason to believe there is a source

inside the FBI working with the top players in organized crime. This man was working with the Marcheses, but now that they have been arrested, he is likely working with their rival, Johnny Raffa. I was planning to discuss this matter with Jerome Gardner yesterday, I left a phone message for him, but obviously that's impossible now." Wyatt leaned forward. "Are you planning to take on Tony and Franco Marchese as clients? Because if so, you're in danger, too."

Abby found herself holding her breath as Kevin Twain drummed his fingers on the glossy desk while staring at Wyatt.

"I will not be taking Tony and Franco on as clients," he said, breaking the silence.

She tried to mask her disappointment.

"May I ask why not?" Wyatt asked. "Are you handing the case over to an associate, instead?"

"No, our firm is no longer representing either man." Kevin Twain paused, then added, "I learned this morning that they were found dead in their respective jail cells."

She sucked in a harsh breath. "Dead? When? How?"

Attorney Twain glanced at her, then back at Wyatt. "Supposedly they committed suicide. But based on what I'm hearing now, I'm sure they were murdered. Just like my partner, Jerry."

"Would you be willing to share any information your partner may have gotten from the Marcheses? I'm mostly interested if they mentioned working with someone specific within the Bureau. Obviously, whoever is involved is ruthlessly killing anyone who may threaten to expose him."

Twain grimaced. "I wish I could, but attorney-client privilege remains even after death." He hesitated, then added, "I will tell you that Jerry never mentioned anything like that to me. We had status update meetings once a week, and if that was something he was aware of, he would have mentioned it, because it would have impacted how he was handling their cases."

"Thank you for letting me know." Wyatt reached across the desk to grab a pen and sticky note. "I'm going to leave my phone number with you, and that of Sheriff Liam Harland from Green Lake, Wisconsin. If you find anything within Jerry's notes about a source inside law enforcement, federal or local, I would appreciate knowing that." He sighed. "I want to prevent anyone else from being murdered."

Kevin Twain nodded, reaching for the note.

"I will. There may be a way around the privilege if I find evidence of an ongoing crime."

"Thanks." Wyatt glanced at her and stood. She followed suit. "Again, we appreciate your time."

Kevin stood, too, but called out as they headed for the door. "Agent Kane? Be careful."

Wyatt glanced somberly over his shoulder. "We will."

"I can't believe they're dead," she whispered as they rode the elevator back down to the lobby level.

"Yeah, although I shouldn't be surprised." He took her hand. "Anyone ruthless enough to kill a lawyer isn't going to balk at killing two prisoners."

"I get it, but how are we going to get the proof you need?" She tried not to sound as dejected as she felt. For every step forward, they were shoved three steps back. At this rate, they'd never get to the truth.

"We'll find a way. I also think Kevin Twain will go through Jerome's files. If there's something in there, I'm confident he'll let us know."

She hoped he was right. When they reached the lobby, Wyatt held her back long enough to scan the area for threats. Then he tugged on her hand, indicating she could step out.

"Okay, I need to make sure the hoodie guy isn't still outside." Wyatt kept his tone low, as there were other people in the lobby now, all dressed professionally, which would help the hoodie guy stand out. "Stay behind me."

"I will." Releasing his hand, she latched on to the back of his jacket. She was keenly aware of how several of the pedestrians in the lobby looked curiously at them.

So much for trying to keep a low profile.

Her pulse kicked up as Wyatt headed to the side entrance they'd used just fifteen minutes ago.

It had only taken a quarter of an hour for their quest for truth to hit a brick wall.

Wyatt stayed to one side as he peered through the glass door. A second later, he gently pushed her backward. "He's still out there."

Not good. Wyatt eased her away from the door to the main lobby. This time, he went in the opposite direction, to the northern doorway.

She held her breath as he slipped up to the door and peered out. Long seconds passed before he turned to glance at her.

"I don't see anyone lurking nearby, but that

doesn't mean much. Once we're outside, we need to blend into the crowd as soon as possible."

"Understood." She steadied her nerves. "Ready when you are."

He looked again for a long moment before pushing the door open. Still holding tightly to his jacket, she followed.

They'd only taken a few steps before Wyatt urgently whispered, "Run!"

The sidewalk to their right contained several people, so she didn't hesitate to head that way.

Desperately praying there wouldn't be another crack of gunfire.

The moment Wyatt caught a glimpse of a man wearing a black leather jacket, he realized the entire office building had been under surveillance from all sides.

Keeping himself behind Abby, he all but pushed her toward the crowded sidewalk.

He heard the pounding of footsteps behind him. Rather than shooting at them, the leather jacket guy was following!

"He's behind us. Find another building."

Abby nodded and picked up the pace. Thankfully, she was fast and easily wove between pedestrians. Several complained loudly, but they ignored the irate comments.

Abby made an abrupt turn into another office building. Wyatt quickly followed her lead.

"This way." He gestured for her to head straight to the back of the building. She didn't hesitate to push through the door. Close on her heels, he glanced around. There was no sign of hoodie or leather jacket yet, but he had to assume there were two other unknown assailants out there. There had likely been four guys total watching each side of the Dettmer office building.

They couldn't slow down now.

Abby read his mind about the need to keep moving. She quickly turned right to join another group of pedestrians.

"Keep up the good work," he whispered as they merged with the others.

She nodded and broke into a run. He remained close behind her, wishing he could wrap her in bulletproof gear from head to toe.

Abby darted into a restaurant next, leading him through the kitchen. He was glad she was experienced in evasive techniques, no doubt learned from her father over the years.

"We can't stop yet," he urged as they continued along another sidewalk. He tried to bring a map of downtown Chicago to the forefront of his mind. "There's a park up on the left. That will be a good place to look for a taxi."

"Okay." She sounded breathless but didn't slow down. He risked a glance over his shoulder.

From what he could see, no one was following them.

So far, so good.

Abby put on a burst of speed to get through the next crosswalk. Then she veered to the left.

The park wasn't big enough to hide in for long. He followed Abby to the other side, where she finally slowed down.

"Is this okay?" she asked, between gulping breaths.

"Yeah." He quickly scanned the street. The good thing about Chicago was there were always cabs around. "Up ahead, see the taxi? Let's grab it."

She nodded and rushed forward, raising her arm to grab the driver's attention. He nodded and eased forward. Then he unlocked the doors.

Abby scrambled inside as Wyatt slid in right next to her. "Can you take us to the Fresh Family Restaurant?" He thought for a minute, then added the address. "And there's no rush."

"Of course." The driver glanced at them in his rearview mirror, obviously curious about the sweat beading their brow from their mad race through the city followed by the lack of urgency in getting to the restaurant.

He wasn't about to explain.

"Thank you." For the first time since leaving the Dettmer office building, Wyatt relaxed against the seat.

They'd made it!

Abby leaned close, speaking in his ear. "All that and we haven't learned anything helpful."

"I know." He understood and shared her frustration. With Tony and Franco dead, his boss could continue with business as usual.

He couldn't keep investigating the case alone for much longer. At some point, he'd have to trust Larry Turks, Special Agent in Charge of the Chicago office.

Yet, without something tangible, he feared Turks would ignore him. Or worse, believe Hawthorne's lies that he was the one taking money from the Marchese crime family.

It was difficult to prove a negative. Especially now that both Marchese men were dead.

His only hope was to find Abby's father. Something he knew she wanted, too.

And if that didn't work?

No, don't go there. He straightened in his seat, refusing to accept defeat. They would find Peter Miller.

They had to find him.

When the taxi driver stopped at the next light, he caught a glimpse of the guy wearing a black leather jacket. He turned his back toward the window, cupped Abby's head and drew her in for a kiss.

She seemed surprised but melted against him in a way that made his head spin. On some distant level he knew she'd be upset that he'd kissed her to hide their faces from leather jacket guy, but that wasn't enough to make him stop.

He'd dreamed of kissing her again since yesterday.

He didn't want to ever stop.

The taxi lurched forward. He forced himself to break off from the kiss, but continued holding Abby close.

"Don't be mad, but I caught a glimpse of leather jacket guy at the intersection back there."

Despite his request not to be angry, she stiffened. "That's why you kissed me?"

"Abby." He lifted her chin with his finger. "I always want to kiss you. But yes, the timing was because of the guy. I assume the men who were watching the office building spread out to see if they could find us."

She stared, her bright blue gaze accusing. "You could have told me so I could hide my face against your chest."

"Yeah, I could have." He shrugged, the corner of his mouth quirking up in a smile. "But kissing you was more fun."

"This isn't about fun!" She kept her voice low so the driver couldn't hear. "Next time let me know what's going on!"

"Okay, I hear you." A pang of regret hit hard. Maybe she hadn't enjoyed the kiss as much as he had. Although her response to the kiss seemed to indicate otherwise. "I'm sorry. I shouldn't have taken advantage of the situation."

"It's fine."

He risked a glance through both side windows, but didn't see hoodie or leather jacket. He hoped that meant they'd lost them.

"Excuse me, would you mind heading to a hotel, instead?" Wyatt met the driver's gaze. "It's about five miles from here." He gave him the name of the hotel where they'd spent the night.

"Sure, why not?" The man smirked as if imagining the were heading there for a quick liaison. Wyatt didn't intend to correct his erroneous assumption.

"Thanks." Wyatt lowered his mouth toward Abby's ear. "We'll get another taxi from the hotel to the restaurant, just to be on the safe side."

"Fine with me." She peered around him to look out the window, too. "I assume it's safe to sit back now?"

"Ah, yeah." He reluctantly released her. If the driver noticed the sudden coolness between them, he didn't comment.

When they reached the hotel, he paid the man in cash, including a large tip. He also surreptitiously keyed in the 800 number painted on the side of the taxi. Once the driver left, he drew Abby toward the side of the building.

"We need to wait a few minutes before calling another taxi, or the same guy might show up." He showed her his phone. "I took down the toll-free number."

"I understand." She didn't look him directly in the eye, her gaze focused on the traffic moving up and down the street. "I hope the SUV is safe," she added. "We weren't planning to leave it at the restaurant for this long."

"I know." It would put a serious dent in his

cash reserves if he had to get the vehicle out of a boot, a contraption used by the city to lock up car tires of vehicles illegally parked. It was easier than towing them to another location and cost a couple of hundred bucks to get removed.

He forced himself to wait at least fifteen minutes before calling the number to request a taxi. He was promised one would arrive in five to ten minutes.

"I can't wait to get out of Chicago," Abby said. "I hope these guys don't follow us all the way back to Green Lake."

"We should be safe once we're on the interstate." Even as he spoke, he continued watching for potential threats. "They staked out the Dettmer office building because they don't have our vehicle information." He grimaced. "And they knew we'd show up there to talk to Kevin Twain."

"That's somewhat reassuring." She frowned. "I just hope he's not in danger."

"I don't think he's a target now that Tony and Franco are dead." He saw a taxi two blocks down, making its way toward them. "Here's our ride."

Thankfully, this driver was a woman. He opened the door for Abby, then scooted in beside her. He asked the driver to take them to the Fresh Family Restaurant, and she seemed to know right where it was.

Wyatt wished he could relax, but his nerves were still on edge. Seeing the leather jacket guy so far from the Dettmer office building made him wonder how far the men, all four of them he assumed, had spread out their search.

Traffic was its usual mess. Their driver was more conservative in threading through the vehicles, unlike most taxi drivers in the city.

When he finally saw the restaurant up ahead, he considered asking the driver to let them out here so they could walk the rest of the way.

Then changed his mind. Better to remain in the taxi for as long as possible.

The driver pulled into the parking lot of the restaurant. He paid her, then followed Abby out of the car.

To his relief, no boot was on their vehicle. Still, the restaurant wasn't nearly as far from the office building as he'd have liked.

"Get in. I need a minute to check it out."

"Okay." She didn't argue.

After glancing around one last time, he searched for a tracking device. He made his way to the front of the car, and froze when he saw it.

Pulling the device off the vehicle, he stared

in shock. Somehow the men outside the office building had discovered this was their vehicle. How, he had no idea.

He quickly attached the device to another car, then got behind the wheel. "We need to get out of here."

"Why?" Abby's eyes widened with concern.

"Those guys from the office building put a tracker on the car. They know what we're driving." He quickly backed out of the parking spot and merged into traffic.

How long before he picked up a tail? Moving the tracker wasn't enough, not if they had his plate number.

He needed a plan, ASAP. Before more bullets began to fly.

NINE

"How did they know what we were driving?" After escaping the four men stationed around the Dettmer office building, Abby had hoped they would be able to head straight to Green Lake to find her father.

Obviously, she'd been wrong.

"I don't know for sure, but the Wisconsin license plates may have been a clue." His expression was grim as he navigated toward the interstate. "They may have decided to track several cars, figuring we'd be in one of them. They also knew we went to the office building on foot. It's not a stretch for them to think the SUV belonged to us. Especially if they had someone run the plates to discover it's registered to Green Lake County. Unfortunately, my boss has many resources at his disposal."

She swallowed hard, the very real threat they were facing overshadowing her annoyance over the way he'd kissed her. "What can we do? Ditch the car?"

"It might be better to swap the license plate with another SUV." Wyatt glanced at her. "I don't want to waste our cash to buy a replacement."

"We can ask Liam for help."

"I'm not going to risk bringing more bad guys all the way to Green Lake." Wyatt sighed, then added, "Not on purpose, anyway. I'll find someplace to get a new license plate once we're back in Wisconsin."

"Maybe it's better to do that here, in Illinois," she pointed out. "That way the tolls won't register this license plate number at all."

He nodded slowly. "That's a good point. I guess that means we should head for the airport."

"That's a good idea. By the time they discover a plate missing, we'll be long gone."

"That's the goal." He flashed a wry grin. "Never thought I'd be the one breaking the law."

"It's for a good reason." She reached over to squeeze his arm. As much as she'd been hurt by knowing he'd only kissed her to hide their faces, she couldn't stay mad at him. Especially when he claimed he always wanted to kiss her. She felt herself blush, and did her best to stay focused. "I know you wouldn't normally do this sort of thing."

"No, I wouldn't." He hesitated, then said, "My dad was an FBI agent, too. His father, my grandfather, was a cop. We have a long-standing history of working for the good guys. I guess that's a big part of the reason I was so upset to be accused of being dirty. As if I'd betrayed your father by ratting him out to the Mancheses."

"I don't blame you." She could only imagine how difficult that would be. "What does your father think?"

"He died last year of a heart attack." Wyatt sighed. "My mother is seeing someone new, and I'm happy for her. I miss my father's wise counsel, but honestly, I'm glad he's not here to see this. My reputation being put in question would have been difficult for him."

"I'm sorry for your loss. My mom died without me ever getting to know her." She thought of Rachel, who hadn't had the benefit of growing up with her father, either. "Some-times it's hard to understand why we lose the people we love. I guess we need to trust in God's plan."

"We do, but we are also human." He shrugged. "Saying the words is easy, the hard part is to open your heart while listening to

guys stationed outside the law office, her
d kept returning to Wyatt's kiss.

e'd mentioned his parents, but not a
an. Because he didn't have someone spe-
in his life? Or because he hadn't bothered
ention her?

little late to be thinking about the pos-
ity that she'd kissed a man who was in a
ionship. Although it would be better to
now, than later. "You live alone?"

es." He shot her a look of surprise, then
standing dawned. "I'm not married, en-
d or in a relationship. At least, not any-
. I had a fiancée, but she wanted me to
up my career. I was going to do that
, but then the Marchese crime family
egan to heat up, and your father called
anted to help provide information, so
d." He grimaced. "Emma didn't take
In hindsight, it was the right decision
to move on. I have a feeling our rela-
wouldn't have lasted, anyway."

lly? Why not?"

hifted uncomfortably in his seat.
looked for happiness in the wrong
verything I tried to do for her wasn'
ough. I think she thought gett
would make her happy, but he
ess came from within her, r.

God's word. And having faith that He knows
what is best for us."

She eyed him curiously. "You really believe that."

"Yes." His simple answer was touching.
"I've been leaning on my faith since the night
your father was almost killed. That's when I
knew that something was rotten in the organized crime division of the FBI."

"And you set out to make things right," she
reminded him.

"I hope I can." For the first time, he didn't
speak with his usual confidence.

"You will." She tried to settle back in her
seat, but it wasn't easy to relax. Even though
they didn't have the tracker on their car, she
worried the bad guys were still back there,
following them.

Taking the detour to Chicago's O'Hare airport would help. Wyatt chose to travel the
back highways northwest to the large interna-
tional airport. When they reached the travel
hub, he headed to the long-term parking lot.

Her muscles tensed as he drove up and
down each row, carefully searching for a suit-
able license plate. After a few minutes, he
pulled into an empty spot.

"Wait here." He dug in his pocket and
pulled out a pocketknife. He opened it to re-

veal a screwdriver attachment. "This won't take long."

"Okay." She glanced around, taking note of the several security cameras dotting the lot. Wyatt must have noticed them, too, because he'd chosen a location halfway between the cameras. And he'd parked alongside a boxy van.

Hopefully, by the time the bad guys viewed the video footage, they'd have enough to bring them down.

Although she was worried, deep in her gut, that they would never find the proof they so desperately needed. Her father may have some insight to share, but did he have enough to point directly at Wyatt's boss, Ethan Hawthorne?

Probably not.

The license plate swap did not take long. Wyatt returned to the driver's seat and started the engine. "This should buy us some time. Once we get to Green Lake, we may be able to obtain a different vehicle."

"I hope so." Even with the incognito license plate, she again found it difficult to relax. As Wyatt headed north to the interstate that would take them to Wisconsin, she glanced over her shoulder at the traffic behind them, half expecting either the bad guys

to show up, or the police to pu for stealing.

By the time they reached th state line, she was able to relax a better chance of getting the or other local police to listen t the story. And they could use I rett's names as law enforcem if needed.

When Wyatt got off the i frowned. "What are you doir us all the way to Green Lake.

"I know, but if we're goin to the burned remains of the better to approach from a diff He glanced at her. "My plan west side of the state, then t the center."

Abby swallowed a gro path would take far longer "Okay. But we may need to eat from a fast-food re lieve I'm saying this, but

"Running from bad g ergy, so I can totally re "We'll grab something

She stared out the w to everything they'd all the close calls of

the min

H won cial to m

A sibil relat kno

"Y unde gage more give for h case and w I stay it well for he tionshi

"Rea He "Emma places. good e married of happi

me." He waved a hand impatiently. "I'm not explaining this well, but the truth is, my former fiancée was looking for something I couldn't give her. Something she had to discover within herself."

Her heart ached for him at the same time she was deeply relieved he wasn't involved with Emma any longer. "I'm sorry you had to go through that."

"I'm not." He flashed a smile. "It was all part of God's plan, remember?"

She couldn't help smiling back. "Very true." Her mood turned serious. "I'm grateful God brought you here, Wyatt. I know I didn't trust you at first, and I'm sorry I tossed that log at you. I know I wouldn't have made it this long without your help."

"You're a smart woman. I have no doubt you'd have done fine flying under the radar." He reached over to take her hand. "We'll get through this, Abby. You'll see."

"I know we will." She felt a renewed sense of hope. Swapping the license plates had worked so far. She was confident they'd get to the farmhouse on Duncan Lane without the bad guys finding them.

Wyatt drove into the parking lot of a local fast-food restaurant. "We should head inside to use the facilities and place our order."

"Agree." She didn't mind having the opportunity to stretch her legs. They'd been in a car for what seemed like forever.

Soon they were seated at a small table near the doorway. This time, she reached for his hand.

"I'd like to say grace," she whispered, conscious of the other patrons in the restaurant. She lowered her head and said, "Dear Lord, we thank You for this food and for the way You have graciously kept us safe in Your care. Amen."

"Amen," Wyatt echoed. He held her hand for a long moment, until she met his gaze. "That was beautiful, Abby."

She blushed. "I only reiterated what I learned from you."

He surprised her by lifting her hand and brushing a chaste kiss across her knuckles. "God is always listening," he murmured before releasing her.

Her skin tingled from his touch. She popped a French fry into her mouth as a distraction. "How far away are we from Green Lake?"

"Less than an hour." He dug into his meal with gusto. "I noticed dark clouds moving in, though, so we should expect rain at some point later this evening."

She wrinkled her nose. "I hope it holds off until after we check the farmhouse."

"Me, too."

Eating their meals didn't take long. Back on the road, she took a moment to study the landmarks, in case she needed to come this way, again.

After an hour, Wyatt pulled off the road, parking beneath several large trees with leaves a dazzling yellow color. "We'll walk from here."

"Okay." She wasn't about to complain. The air was heavy with moisture as they cut through a large field to approach the house from the back. The overgrown weeds proved no one had farmed the acreage recently.

Soon the charred walls of the farmhouse came into view. Wyatt put a hand on her arm, drawing her to a crouch. He didn't say anything but she understood he wanted to watch the area before getting too close.

As she knelt there, she lifted her heart in prayer. *Please, Lord, please help us find my dad!*

Wyatt didn't see any sign of recent activity near the farmhouse, but he waited anyway, determined not to be drawn into a trap.

The near miss outside the Dettmer office

building still haunted him. He almost considered calling his partner, Allan, for additional help. It was only his concern that Allan wouldn't believe their boss was dirty that had held him back from making the call.

Soon, though, he may not have a choice. He'd have to trust someone within the Chicago office. But not yet.

He really wanted to find Abby's father first.

They stayed hidden in the weeds for another few minutes before he took Abby's hand and rose to his feet. "Slowly," he cautioned as they began their approach.

She nodded without saying anything. He gave her credit for not rushing forward in her haste to locate her father. If the situation were reversed, he'd have found it difficult to wait as patiently as she had.

He listened intently as the crossed the field. The jagged edges of the walls looked the same as the last time he'd seen them.

"This way," he whispered, lightly steering her to the right, so they could head around the building to reach the front. He paused at the corner, though, and took a moment to make sure there weren't any vehicles in the driveway.

He didn't see anything, or anyone. Which was both good and bad.

How was Peter Miller traveling? On foot? Motorcycle? Car?

There was no way to know for sure. If Abby's dad was on foot, though, he could very well be hiding someplace nearby.

Or he may have already moved on to another place.

The thought of Abby's father watching from afar made him pause. Peter wouldn't know he could trust Wyatt, the way Abby did. If her father saw the two of them together, he may just remain out of sight.

"You should go first," he said in a low voice. "I'll stay here."

She shot him a questioning look. "Are you sure?"

No, he wasn't sure. He didn't like the idea of putting her in danger. "Yeah, but don't go too far down the driveway toward the road. We haven't been able to clear it."

"Okay." She waited a beat, then stood and made her way around the corner. Wyatt rested his hand on his weapon, watching for any sign of movement, either from the bad guys or from Abby's father.

Hopefully, Abby's father. He had no idea where they'd go next if they didn't find him here.

Abby's progress was slow as she carefully

stepped through the ruins. She sent several glances toward the driveway, as if expecting the bad guys to come flying up toward the house, guns blazing. After several minutes, she seemed to focus her attention on what was left of the farmhouse.

When she disappeared from his line of sight, though, he panicked. Rather than calling out to her, he eased around the corner to get a better view.

And when he still couldn't hear her, he ground his teeth together and made his way closer still. There was a gaping hole where the front door would have been located, so he assumed she went inside.

Most of the roof was missing, so lumber falling on her head wasn't a risk, but the walls were half gone. As if on cue, the wind picked up, bringing more dark clouds overhead.

He wanted to trust her instincts, but didn't like the idea of Abby poking around and exploring too far inside the remains, especially considering the dim lighting. He edged closer to the open doorway, glancing once more over his shoulder to see if anyone else was around.

The fact that Abby's father hadn't shown up yet made him worry they'd missed him. Or maybe he'd never been there at all.

He'd stressed that Abby should remain positive, but he knew there was a chance her father had already been taken out of the picture.

Glancing down, he noticed there were soft spots on the wooden porch, evidence of wood rotting from beneath. He stayed close to the more solid edges as he made his way through the opening, wrinkling his nose at the scent of charred wood intermingled with smoke.

"Abby?"

"I'm okay, but you might want to stay back. The floor is not in good shape."

"No kidding, which means you shouldn't be in here, either." He halted his progress, knowing he weighed far more than she did. "Find anything?"

"Not yet."

Based on the condition of the floor, Wyatt didn't think it likely that Abby's father would have risked coming inside. He was about to tell Abby that, urging her to come back, when he heard a creaking noise.

"No!" Abby cried out as he heard a thudding sound.

"Abby? What happened? Where are you?" He peered through the blackened walls.

"I'm okay, just broke through the floor." Her voice sounded strained, as if she might be injured.

"Where are you?" He tested the floor with one foot before moving forward.

"Hold on, I'm okay." He heard scuffling sounds. "Thankfully, I didn't fall all the way through to the basement."

He drew in a harsh breath, but then let it out slowly. Yelling wouldn't do any good. "You need to make your way back here, Abby. Don't go any further."

"Okay, I won't."

He still wasn't satisfied and took another step into the room. Then one more. Imagining the open basement below them wasn't at all reassuring. But he couldn't just leave her to manage on her own, either. "Abby, listen, you might want to crawl out on your hands and knees. That will distribute your weight over a larger area. It may help prevent you from falling through another rotten part of the floor."

"I will, but you need to stay back, Wyatt. It won't help me if you fall through, too."

Staying back wasn't easy, but he forced himself to do just that. After a few minutes he heard her gasp.

"What is it?"

"My dad was here, Wyatt. And recently."

He frowned. "How do you know?"

"Someone used charcoal from the charred

wood to write the word *safe* on the bedroom wall."

"How do you know that your father wrote that?" He wished he could see it for himself.

"I know he did." She sounded breathless now, as if she'd run a marathon. "This was my bedroom when we stayed here all those years ago. I think he came here looking for me. And when I wasn't here, he left a message only I would find."

He wanted to believe her, but it seemed strange that her father would only write one word.

Safe.

Did that mean he was safe? Or that he should keep Abby safe? Maybe both?

Either way, twenty-four hours had passed and they were still no closer to finding him.

TEN

"We need to get out of here, before you fall through more rotted flooring."

She knew Wyatt was right, but was reluctant to leave. Her dad had been in these ruins. He'd written the word *safe*. She lightly touched the wall where the word had been scrawled, as if she could connect with her father. Then she scanned the area, searching for more clues that he may have left for her.

There was nothing. If her dad had time to write the word safe, why hadn't he written more?

Because he'd feared that he'd been followed?

A chill snaked down her spine.

"Abby?" Wyatt sounded impatient.

"Coming." Suppressing a sigh, she retraced her steps to the main area. She gave the area where she'd fallen through a wide berth, testing the flooring before moving forward. Her ankle and knee throbbed a bit from her partial fall but she ignored the pain.

"Let's get out of here."

"Right behind you." With Wyatt preceding her, they made their way carefully around the burned wreckage, the word *safe* embedded in her mind.

Abby knew her father had written the note, but she wished he'd added more clarity. She felt certain he had been telling her that he was safe, but why hadn't he given her an indication of where he was? Or even better, call her on their disposable phones?

Even if he'd lost his old phone, they'd always made it a practice to memorize the numbers so they could simply get a replacement. But her dad hadn't done that. Or if he had, he hadn't reached out to her. Which was highly unusual.

Wyatt paused near a trio of trees sporting colorful leaves. "I guess it's good to know your father was here."

"Yes, but we still don't know where he is now." She huddled beside him, chilled by the wind. "I have no idea where to search next. This farmhouse was our first safehouse after leaving the Amish. The cabin in the woods, where you found me, was our second." As soon as she said the words, an idea formed in her mind. "Wait a minute, we need to check the abandoned cabin where the Marchese men had stashed Rachel. Maybe my dad knows about that place, too."

Wyatt frowned. "What are you talking about? What cabin?"

"The day I was able to help rescue Rachel after she was kidnapped by Franco Marchese, she was being held in a cabin in the northwest corner of Green Lake County." She tried to think back, envisioning the area in her mind. "I'm pretty sure I can find it again."

"It's worth a try," Wyatt agreed.

He turned to leave, but she grabbed his arm. "Is that a car engine?"

Wyatt spun, pulling her down behind the trees. As they listened intently, there was no mistaking the faint rumble of a motor.

"My dad?" she whispered. It was possible her father had gotten hold of a vehicle. She hadn't seen one near the cabin, but he may have had it well hidden. He may be coming back to see if she'd gotten there. The possibility made her wish she'd written a response to his note.

Wyatt considered her thought, then bent to speak in her ear. "Stay here, I'll check it out."

"No, I'll go." She tightened her grip on his arm. "If it's my dad, he'll trust me, Wyatt. Not you."

Frustration flashed in his eyes, but he reluctantly nodded in agreement. She breathed a sigh of relief, then rose to a crouch and ran lightly through the weeds to the back corner of the burned house.

When she paused at the corner, the car engine was louder now. From what she could hear, the vehicle was rocking and rolling over the ruts in the overgrown driveway.

The sound made her hesitate. Would her father drive all the way up the driveway? Or would he park closer to the road and come in on foot, the way she and Wyatt had done? Granted, they had come through the back fields rather than the front of the house, but still, the thought of her dad coming all the way up to the ruin in his vehicle didn't seem right.

She glanced back at Wyatt to find him watching her intently, poised to rush forward at a moment's notice. He rested his hand on the butt of his gun, ready for anything.

Keeping her head down, she inched along the side of the house. She needed to know for sure the driver of the vehicle wasn't her dad.

When she grew closer to the front corner of the building, the car engine abruptly shut off. She froze, listening intently.

There was nothing but silence for a long

moment. She edged closer, then took a quick peek around the corner.

Not her dad, but two men. Dressed in black. Carrying guns.

Her pulse spiked. She needed to get out of here, now! She slipped back along the side of the house, glancing frantically back at Wyatt.

He seemed to sense her concern. She lifted her hand and wrote 9-1-1 in the air. The men in the front of the abandoned farmhouse spoke in curt tones.

"You take the inside, I'll check around back," a deep male voice said.

"It doesn't look safe," the second man complained.

Abby knew she was running out of time. One or both gunmen would round the corner of the house any moment. She continued moving quickly, debating on giving up silence for speed.

Wyatt had his gun in his hand now, but she couldn't tell if he'd called 911 to update the sheriff's department. When she heard the first guy agree to go inside the burned wreckage, she knew there was no choice but to run.

Up ahead, Wyatt moved to the opposite side of the three trees, staying somewhat behind the largest one, his gun raised, clearly anticipating one of the bad guys would show up.

She sprinted toward him, flinching as the crack of gunfire echoed around her. Knowing she was being shot at only made her put on another burst of speed.

Wyatt fired in response, providing the time she needed to reach him. She dove toward the protection of the trees, keeping her head down as more gunfire reverberated around her.

These were serious bad guys.

Another shout and a crashing noise reached them. She wasn't sure what had happened but thought maybe the gunman inside the house had also partially fallen through the rotted floor, the way she had. If so, she hoped and prayed he'd be stuck there for a few minutes.

Drawing in a deep breath, she scrambled behind Wyatt. "Are you okay?"

"Fine, you?" He didn't take his eyes off the gunman who was now seeking shelter behind the ruins.

She didn't feel any pain, not even in her ankle and knee. "I'm good. Did you call 911?"

"I called Liam directly, but have no clue how long it will take for them to get here."

"There are two gunmen. One went inside the house. I think he's the one who cried out in pain from falling through the floor. I'm sure it won't take him long to get free. He'll probably join this guy any minute."

As she spoke, another gunshot rang out. This time, hitting the bark of the tree near Wyatt's head. She sucked in a harsh breath, waves of fear washing over her. Wyatt would be facing two gunmen with only one weapon.

Please, Lord, keep us safe in Your care!

Wyatt hadn't heard the second gunman since the cry and crashing sound had come from within the ruins. But as Abby pointed out, the man would get himself free soon enough. Keeping one eye on the far corner of the house, he waited for the initial hit man to show himself.

For long seconds, there was nothing but silence.

Then he saw a face and an arm emerge from the spot Abby had been just a few minutes earlier. Without hesitation, he fired again, and this time, the guy cried out in pain.

The gun dropped from the guy's hand, and he went down on one knee, grabbing his injured arm. Wyatt almost thought it was a ruse to draw him out, but then he saw the blood running down the attacker's arm.

There was still no sign of the second gunman, but he couldn't wait any longer. Wyatt rushed out from behind the trees, heading directly toward the injured gunman, his weapon trained on the guy's head.

"FBI! Don't move!" he barked. When he was close enough, he kicked the gun out of the way, then knelt on the ground beside the injured man. Quickly holstering his own weapon, he grabbed the shooter's wrists, ignoring a howl of pain as he drew them together behind his back.

"Who are you? Who sent you?" Wyatt took off his jacket and used the sleeve to bind the man's wrists together as he scanned the area, searching for the second attacker.

"You're hurting me," the guy whined.

Abby appeared beside him, holding the gunman's weapon. He should have known she wouldn't stay back. And really, he didn't mind having a partner since there was one perp unaccounted for.

"Cover him. I'm going to find the second gunman."

"Got it," Abby said curtly.

He had the fleeting thought she'd make a good cop, as he rose and began moving cautiously along the back side of the farmhouse. He'd decided to head in the opposite direction from where Abby and the wounded man were located, assuming this was where the second gunman would have come.

When he reached the corner, though, he didn't see anyone. Knowing the perp could be hiding, he took his time scanning the area. But there was no hint of movement.

He sent up a silent prayer asking for God to protect him and Abby, before making his way around the corner. Moving fast now, he ran toward the front of the farmhouse.

A black sedan was in the driveway, but again there was no sign of the second man. He didn't like being out in the open like this. The guy could be hiding anywhere, waiting for the perfect opportunity to make his move.

He crouched down behind the front of the sedan, noting the engine under the hood was still warm. These guys must have driven for a while, maybe even all the way from Chicago.

How had they found this place? He'd have to question the injured man, as soon as he'd neutralized the second gunman.

After hearing no further sounds, he decided to keep going. In a swift move, he leaped to his feet and darted up to the rotted porch, stepping along the edges the way he'd done earlier. Once he was behind a partial wall he paused and looked down at the floorboards. He didn't want to fall through the way Abby had.

The way the second gunman might have.

There were dozens of scuff marks on what remained of the floor. He glanced around, trying to anticipate where the second man had gone first.

Since this area of the house was fairly open, Wyatt had to assume the perp had gone down the short hallway to the bedrooms. He took his time testing the floorboards, before putting his entire weight on them.

He'd only gone a few feet, when he saw a large gaping hole in the floor. One that had not been there earlier.

He went down on his hands and knees, then stretched out on his belly to distribute his weight. Inching across the floor wasn't easy, but he finally reached the edge of the opening.

It was too dark to see anything, so he shifted around until he could bring up his phone. Even cheap phones had screens that would light up.

Aiming the screen through the opening, he saw a man lying face down on the ground. The guy didn't move or make a single sound.

Was he dead? Or just knocked unconscious?

Wyatt risked moving closer to the edge of the opening, praying the boards would hold his weight. Using his phone screen as a light, he took another look, and this time, he noticed the gunman's weapon was lying way off to the side.

And there was a charred two-by-four beneath his head, blood pooling in the dirt.

He watched for long moments, before determining the guy was not breathing. Wyatt felt sure the man had either sustained a deadly concussion or broken his neck during the fall.

Liam and his deputies would be able to find out for sure. Regardless, this gunman was no longer a threat to him or to Abby. Even if he managed to survive and get to his feet, there was no easy way for him to climb out of the basement.

They were safe, but he didn't like losing one of the culprits like this. It would have been more helpful to interrogate them about who'd hired them and why.

Now there was only one man to question. If he'd even talk. Which Wyatt wasn't at all convinced he would.

Police sirens echoed through the ruins. Thankfully, Liam and his deputies were on their way. Wyatt inched back away from the gaping hole toward the front of the farmhouse.

Abby hadn't made a sound and, surprisingly, neither had the wounded gunman. Now that the threat was over, he called out to reassure her.

"Abby, I found the second guy. He fell all

the way through the floor to the basement. He's not moving, and I can't see that he's breathing, either."

"Be careful," Abby cautioned. "All that walking on the floor may have caused more damage than we realized. There may be more weak areas than there were before."

No kidding, he thought wryly. "I'm okay, moving very slowly to be safe. Just keep your weapon trained on our perp."

"I will, but Wyatt, this guy is bleeding pretty badly from his wound. The bullet may have nicked an artery. I'm trying to hold pressure, but it's not looking good."

No! They couldn't lose their only lead! They needed the gunman alive and talking.

"Keep holding pressure, I'm coming." He wanted to jump up and run, but forced himself to continue his painstakingly slow process of inching across the floor in a sol-dier-like belly crawl. The sirens grew louder, making it harder to hear creaking or poten-tially breaking boards beneath him.

It seemed to take forever, but soon he felt the cold wind brushing along the back of his neck. No rain yet, thankfully. When he fi-nally made it all the way to the porch, he pushed himself upright. Ignoring the way his clothes and hands were covered in soot and dust, he rushed over to where Abby knelt beside the wounded man. She had the rest of his jacket balled up to help staunch the blood. The guy had his eyes closed and he didn't seem to notice the way Abby was leaning all her weight on his open wound.

No wonder the guy hadn't made a sound. He was hanging on to his life by a thin thread. The lack of color in the man's face was concerning.

"Hey, can you hear me?" Wyatt shook the man's uninjured shoulder. "Look at me."

The gunman's eyes flittered open. Wyatt leaned over so he could stare into the man's dark eyes. "Listen carefully. Your buddy is dead, but we can get you to the hospital very soon. I need to know who you are and who hired you to come after us."

It took a long moment for the injured man's gaze to focus on him. "Help…me."

"Can you hear the sirens? Help is on the way." Wyatt willed the guy to remain conscious. "But you need to tell me who sent you. Who is your contact?"

"Raf…" the man's eyes slowly closed.

"Raffa?" Wyatt shook him again, knowing this might be their one and only chance to get the information they needed. "Did Johnny Raffa hire you?"

The injured man managed a slight nod.

"How did Raffa know we were here?" He shook the guy, and he groaned. The sirens were so loud now that it was hard to hear. Wyatt raised his voice, nearly shouting at the man. "Come on, I need you to help me out. How did Raffa know we were here?"

The sirens abruptly shut off, leaving a loud silence in their wake. Wyatt didn't take his gaze off the injured man's face, unwilling to miss anything, even an attempt to mouth words.

But it was no use. The guy's jaw went slack. Wyatt shook him again, trying to revive him, then stopped, fearing he was only making his injury worse.

"Back here!" he shouted to let the cops know their location. "Threat is neutralized. Repeat, there are no more gunmen to be concerned about."

"Wyatt, is that you?" a familiar voice asked.

"Yes, Liam. I'm here with Abby. One gunman is inside the house. He fell through the basement floor. The other is here, and bleeding badly. We need an ambulance."

"It will be here shortly." Liam stepped around the corner, his gun drawn despite Wyatt's assurances they were fine. He understood the sheriff had to be ready for anything. For all Liam knew, they may have been forced to say those words while being held at gunpoint.

"We're losing him." Abby sent a pleading look at Liam. "Please tell them to hurry. He hasn't told us anything helpful."

Liam came over and knelt near the guy's head. He reached out and rested his fingers along the side of the gunman's neck. After a long moment, he shook his head. "I'm afraid it's too late. He's gone."

"No!" Wyatt immediately placed his hands on the guy's chest and began performing compressions. "We need him. Get the ambulance here!"

Liam turned and gestured for the ambulance crew. They rushed forward and went to work. Wyatt continued chest compressions while they tried to establish an IV line.

But they couldn't do it, and without an IV, they couldn't give him any blood. After ten minutes, even Wyatt had to admit their efforts were useless.

Still, the two EMTs lifted the gunman onto their gurney and hurried him over to the waiting ambulance. The older of the two glanced back over his shoulder. "We'll continue CPR on the way."

Wyatt closed his eyes for a moment, wishing he'd handled this entire confrontation differently. Maybe if he'd fired over his head, the gunman would have surrendered his weapon.

Yet even as the thought formed, he realized it was useless to go back and wish for things to have been different.

The bleak truth was that they'd just lost their best chance of uncovering his boss as a leak within the FBI.

And Wyatt was losing hope they ever would.

ELEVEN

Abby tried to wipe the gunman's blood from her hands on handfuls of leaves from the ground. Although she'd used Wyatt's jacket to hold pressure, the wound had bled out copiously.

"I didn't mean to kill him." Wyatt's low, anguished voice tugged at her heart. "I only wanted to make him stay back, to defend Abby, but he wouldn't stop…"

This was the second time Wyatt had been forced to take a life in their short time together, and she sensed both losses weighed heavily on his shoulders. Not least of all because he was a man of faith.

"I know you didn't." She moved closer and did her best to offer support.

Liam's gaze held empathy. "I don't blame you, Wyatt. You had to react to the threat. Especially since there were two of them."

"Only one man. The other was lying on the basement floor," Wyatt corrected.

"You didn't know that and neither did I. We thought he was hiding, waiting for the right time to begin firing."

"I agree with Abby, that's a reasonable assessment of the situation." Liam clapped Wyatt on the shoulder. "Don't second-guess your instincts."

Wyatt's expression remained grim. "I understand what you're saying, but the point is we needed one of these guys alive. To find out who sent them and how they found us here."

She frowned. "He said Raffa sent him."

"Maybe. But he didn't say the full name of Raffa. We're only speculating that was his intent." Wyatt blew out a breath. "And I wanted to know more about Raffa and how he knew we were here, especially after all the precautions we took to stay under the radar."

"I know you've both had a rough few hours, but I need you to return to Green Lake with me," Liam said. "I need official statements, and it looks as if you both need to get cleaned up."

"Sure." Wyatt still looked troubled. "We'll follow you in the SUV you loaned us." He hesitated, then added, "You should probably know that the license plates are stolen."

Liam's eyebrows rose, but he nodded. "Precautions, huh?"

"We were running from gunmen in Chicago," Abby chimed in. "There's a lot that has happened since we left yesterday."

"I can't wait to hear the entire story," Liam drawled. "But considering you were found here, I think you should leave the borrowed SUV behind. I'll find something else for you to drive once we're finished. Oh, and I'll need to confiscate your weapon, but can give you a replacement so you're not left unarmed."

Abby glanced at Wyatt, who nodded in agreement. "That's fine with me," he said.

"Me, too," Abby agreed.

Fat raindrops began to fall from the dark sky. Wyatt was unusually silent as they rode with Liam back to the sheriff's department headquarters. She excused herself to use the facilities to clean up, while trying to think of where she should go next to find her dad.

She did her best to remove the bloodstains from her jacket and jeans, then headed out to rejoin Liam and Wyatt. She found them in the same conference room they'd used the last time they were here.

Was it really just yesterday morning?

Wyatt had cleaned up, too, but his expression remained somber. She dropped into the seat next to him, then reached out to grasp his hand. He glanced at her, offering a wan smile, then continued filling Liam in on what they'd found in Chicago.

"Franco and Tony Marchese are both dead? Along with their lawyer?" Liam asked incredulously. "No doubt in my mind they'd been silenced to keep the FBI leak a secret."

"I believe so," Wyatt said wearily. "Which is why I'm so upset that we lost both gunmen."

"Not our fault," she quickly reminded him.

"Maybe not, but that doesn't change the end result." He sighed. "I don't suppose you have any intel for us?"

Liam grimaced. "Not yet, but I've asked that we get the fingerprints from the two dead men into the system, ASAP. Their names may help. Oh, the truck was found abandoned at the side of the road, but it was wiped clean."

"Names would be good since the truck is a dead end." Wyatt looked at Liam steadily. "I'm ready to give my statement about what happened at the burned farmhouse."

"Okay. I'll ask Abby to step out." Liam gestured toward the door. "She can give her statement to Garrett."

She clung to Liam's hand for a moment, wishing she didn't have to leave, but knew the sooner they finished, the sooner they'd be back on the road searching for her father.

"Of course." She reluctantly released Liam and stood. When she stepped into the hallway, she saw Garrett standing there. He led her down a hallway to a small office not far from Liam's.

To Garrett's credit he didn't interrupt as she explained how they'd gone to the ruined farmhouse to search for her father. That it was only as they were getting ready to leave that they'd heard a car drive up. She'd gone to investigate, hoping the vehicle was being used by her father, only to find two gunmen, instead.

"Things happened fast," she said. "I tried to sneak away, but knew he would see me, so I ran. I heard a gunshot as I reached the trees. That's when Wyatt returned fire."

"How do you know Wyatt didn't shoot first?" Garrett asked.

She wanted to lash out in anger but forced herself to remain calm, taking a long moment to search her memory about the sequence of events. "I was running toward him at the same time he moved to the side of the trees to make room for me in the sheltered area. After hearing the gunshot, I saw him lift his weapon and fire back. There's no way he took the first shot."

"Okay, that makes sense." She was glad Garrett believed her. Her flash of annoyance must have shown on her face, because he added, "I have to ask these questions, Abby. It's important to get the facts documented correctly."

"I understand." It was clear Garrett was doing his job, just as Liam was doing with Wyatt. It would be important that their stories mesh. "I heard Wyatt shout at him to drop his weapon, but that didn't happen, as a bullet hit the tree trunk inches from us."

"We'll make sure the slug is pulled out of the tree," Garrett said. "Anything else?"

"We went over to provide first aid, then Wyatt headed out to find the second gunman. We heard a crash from within the wreckage, but didn't know that he'd fallen all the way through the floor to the basement."

Garrett nodded and made more notes. "Then what happened?"

She stared down at her hands for a moment. "Wyatt took a long time to clear the area, but once he found the guy lying in the basement, he told me he was no threat, then rushed over to help provide first aid to the injured man. Wyatt asked him questions about who sent him, and he only managed to say *Raf*, which we think means Raffa. When Wyatt asked if Raffa sent him, he nodded. But then he couldn't say anything more. Despite holding pressure on his wound, he bled out anyway."

"I know, he was pronounced dead on arrival to the ER." Garrett gave her a sympathetic look. "Not many people would offer first aid to someone who'd tried to kill them. You did your best, Abby, and so did Wyatt."

They had, but it wasn't quite good enough.

"You have any thoughts as to how they followed you to that location?" Garrett asked.

She slowly shook her head. "We changed, or rather stole a license plate at O'Hare airport to avoid being caught by the toll cameras." She flushed. "We didn't want to break the law, but after being chased by gunmen stationed outside the law office, we felt it necessary to take drastic measures." She frowned. "And they still found us."

"There were probably cameras at O'Hare, too," Garrett said.

"Yes, but we thought we avoided them." She sighed. "Maybe we didn't, and they were still able to track us all the way to Wisconsin."

"And maybe they just assumed you'd go back to that farmhouse," Garrett said. "Maybe Wyatt's boss knows his thought process too well."

Something occurred to her. She didn't know exactly when her dad had been at the farmhouse to write the word *safe* on the wall, but maybe it had been earlier, shortly before the black truck opened fire on her and Wyatt. Maybe her father had been followed there by the two gunmen. "Anything is possible," she murmured, mostly to herself.

"Give me a minute to see if Liam is finished with Wyatt." Garrett stood and left her in the office.

A wave of exhaustion hit hard. The adrenaline that had fueled her earlier had abruptly subsided, leaving her feeling shaky and slightly sick to her stomach.

She'd thought helping her sister, Rachel, to escape and taking down Tony Marchese had been harrowing, but these recent events were worse.

And there was no end in sight.

Surprising how much Wyatt missed having Abby sitting beside him. He'd recited the events that had led to his shooting the gunman, in a clear, concise manner. It was strange to be the one sitting on this side of the interview table, rather than doing the interrogating himself.

The longer it took him to get the evidence

he needed to prove Ethan Hawthorne was dirty, the less likely he'd be able to salvage his career.

Not that keeping his job was as important as saving lives. He'd give it up in a heartbeat to protect Abby and her father.

He was angry that they were in this situation, because Peter had tried to do the right thing by coming forward with information to bring criminals down.

"Can you think of anything else to add?" Liam asked.

He focused on the sheriff. "No, that's everything. But I will take you up on that offer of a replacement vehicle." He winced. "I know it's the second one in two days."

"Not your fault and I don't mind." Liam stood. "We have one more spare vehicle to offer you, a dark gray Jeep. If that one gets burned, we'll have little choice but to provide you one of our personal vehicles."

"No, that would be too dangerous," Wyatt protested. "I wouldn't want your family to be at risk."

"I wouldn't want that, either. My wife, Shauna, is pregnant," Liam confided. "Okay, not a personal vehicle, but we can get something out of Appleton if needed. Oh, and I have a service weapon for you, too."

"Okay, thanks." He took the gun and clip. "Hopefully, this will be the last time I need this sort of favor."

"I'll reach out to the Chicago PD as well, to let them know about the license plate exchange." Liam rose to his feet. "I'll grab the keys to the Jeep."

Roughly five minutes after Liam left, Garrett and Abby came into the room. The chief deputy nodded at him. "Liam was called away, but gave me the keys to the Jeep. Come with me. I'll show you where it's parked."

"Thanks." He reached out to take Abby's hand. "We appreciate all of your help."

"There is one more thing," Garrett said, pausing in the hallway. "We don't have a picture of Abby's father, Peter Miller."

"I don't have one to give you," Abby said. "At least, not with me."

"I understand, but we have a sketch artist who happens to be here regarding another case. Her name is Jacy Urban." Garrett's gaze rested on Abby. "You could describe your father for her."

Abby didn't immediately agree. "Why do you want his picture?"

Garrett looked surprised. "Our deputies are patrolling the entire county. Having a picture of what your father looks like would help us find him."

"He's not going to let himself be seen by the police," she protested.

"Abby, what's the harm in having more eyes out there looking for him?" Garrett searched her gaze. "Maybe they'll see him when they're off duty."

She worried her lower lip with her teeth, before reluctantly nodding. "Fine. I'll work with your sketch artist. I don't think this will help, though. My dad has been avoiding the police for the past eighteen, well, going on nineteen years."

"Thanks, Abby. I know he's a master at staying off grid, but you never know what might happen," Garrett said. "If the danger gets to a certain point, he may come to see us."

"Don't set your hopes on that," Abby said wearily.

Wyatt had his doubts, too, but knew it couldn't hurt to have more people out there searching for her father. He and Abby followed Garrett through the myriad of cubicles until they reached a pretty blonde who had a sketchbook and charcoal pencils before her.

"Jacy, this is Abby Miller and FBI agent Wyatt Kane," Garrett quickly made the intro-

ductions. "We'd like you to work with Abby
to sketch her father."

Jacy's eyes widened in surprise, likely because most people didn't need to sketch their
family members, but nodded. "Of course.
Please take a seat, Abby. Have you worked
with a sketch artist before?"

"No." Abby sat beside Jacy. "But I'm willing to try."

"Great." Jacy picked up a pencil and began
asking questions. She started with the general shape of her dad's face, his hair, his eyes,
his jawline.

Wyatt hadn't worked with a sketch artist in
his role at the Bureau, and found it fascinat-
ing to watch Jacy create the likeness of Peter
Miller on the page. He'd met the man twice
months ago, but Abby was doing a far better
job describing him.

Soon Abby was leaning forward, making small corrections to his nose and mouth.
Then she sat back, eyeing the sketch criti-
cally. "That's my dad."

"You were great, Abby," Jacy said with a
smile. "You know your father's features very
well."

"Thanks." She blushed, then shrugged.
"Truthfully, I haven't seen him for the past

few months, so he may have grown a beard or done something else to change his looks."

"Men tend to grow or remove facial hair, while women dye their hair different colors," Jacy agreed. "But usually, it's a person's eyes that give their identity away."

"I'm sure you're right. Me, my sister, Rachel, and our dad have the same blue eyes." Abby stared at the sketch for a long moment before rising to her feet. "Thanks, Jacy."

"Anytime." Jacy pulled the sketch from the pad. "I'll get this scanned and distributed to the deputies."

"I can do that," Garrett offered. He took the sketch from Jacy, then glanced at Wyatt. "Once I get this scanned, we'll head outside to the Jeep."

Abby still didn't look happy about the image of her father going out to every one of the Green Lake County sheriff's deputies, but she didn't say anything. After Garrett scanned and loaded the image of Peter Miller on a nearby computer, he used the keyboard to send it out to the team.

Abby slipped her hand in Wyatt's. He gave her a reassuring smile. "It's going to be fine."

"I hope so." Her gaze was serious. "I hope they don't treat him as a criminal."

"They won't," Garrett said. "He's a missing person, not a person of interest in a crime."

If anything, Abby looked more alarmed. "You're not going to send out some sort of silver alert, are you? The bad guys will know to come here to find him!"

"No silver alert, no announcement," Garrett hastily promised. "I need you to trust us, Abby. We only want to keep you and your father safe."

As that was Wyatt's mission, too, he added, "And the sooner we find him, the better. We need to reach your father before Raffa's hit men do."

"Okay, okay." She drew in a deep breath and let it out in a rush. "I do trust you, Garrett. Liam, too. It's just…" She hesitated, as if trying to find the right words. "My dad won't trust your deputies, so they need to reassure him that I'm okay, and that their only goal is to reunite us for safety reasons."

"I hear you loud and clear," Garrett said. "I'll emphasize that with my team."

"Good." As he was still holding her hand, he could feel some of the tension ease. "Thank you."

"Come on, let's find that Jeep." Garrett turned away from the computer, but Abby's gaze was locked on the sketch.

"Garrett, can we take that sketch with us?" Wyatt reached out to snag it. "You already have it in your system, right?"

"Right." Garrett shrugged. "Sure, you can have it."

Abby flashed a grateful smile and took the sketch. "I appreciate this."

"Hey, Garrett?" Liam called from his office. "Are Wyatt and Abby still here?"

"Yes, why?" Garrett asked.

"I have news." Liam emerged from his office, a slip of paper in hand. "We have a hit on the fingerprints on the gunman you shot, Wyatt."

"What was his name?" Wyatt was still upset with himself for shooting the guy and hitting his artery. Although after he'd recounted the events for Liam, he'd been forced to admit that given the exact same set of circumstances, he'd do the same thing again.

It was easy to second-guess yourself once you had all the information at your fingertips. But at the time, he hadn't known about the guy falling into the basement. All he knew was that the gunman was shooting at her.

Forcing him to return fire.

"Does the name Rico Vane mean anything to you?" Liam asked.

"No." Wyatt tried not to show his defeat,

but he'd really hoped to recognize the name of one of Johnny Raffa's known associates. "If you found his prints in the system, he must have been arrested at some point. What did he do?"

"He did a year for aggravated assault." Liam grimaced. "I was hoping you'd know more."

"I wish I did. But he must have been working with Raffa. He started to say Raffa's name when I questioned him."

"It's likely," Liam agreed. "I'll give you a call when we have the second gunman's prints entered into the system. That will take some time, though, as he hasn't been extricated from the scene. It stopped raining, but the water pooling on the floor only makes it more treacherous. What is left of the structure is extremely unstable."

Wyatt knew Liam was right to take his time in getting the dead guy out of the basement. He wouldn't want any of the sheriff's deputies to be hurt, either. "Keep me updated."

"I will." Liam stepped back. "Stay safe."

"That's the plan." Wyatt turned to follow Garrett back through the building and out to the Jeep. A minute later, the chief deputy had gone back inside, leaving him and Abby alone.

The way she kept staring at the sketch bothered him. "Abby, is something wrong?"

She shook her head, but then a tear rolled down her cheek. "What if I never see my father again?"

"Hey, don't think the worst." He took the sketch, set it in the Jeep, then pulled her into his arms. "Your dad's message indicated he's safe. We need to have faith that God will watch over him the same way He's watching over us."

Abby slipped her arms around his waist and hugged him tight. He didn't mind holding her; he needed this connection as much as she did.

Maybe more. Because if he were honest, he'd admit he didn't want to let her go.

TWELVE

Abby clung to Wyatt as if he were a lifeboat in a stormy sea. After everything that had happened, she was losing hope.

Losing faith.

She had a very bad feeling she and Wyatt wouldn't find her dad before it was too late.

"Lord Jesus, we pray You keep Abby's dad safe in Your care. Amen," Wyatt whispered.

Despite her fear, she was touched by his prayer. "Amen," she murmured. Gathering her strength, she lifted her head and gazed up at him. "Thank you. That was just what I needed."

The corner of his mouth tipped up in a crooked smile. "The hug or the prayer?"

Despite her earlier despair, she couldn't help smiling back. "Both."

"I'm glad." He stared down at her for a long moment, his gaze lingering on her mouth. She longed for him to kiss her again, but he took a step back and added, "We should go and find a place to stay."

"Okay." She tried to hide her disappointment.

Then Wyatt surprised her by moving close and dropping a quick kiss on her lips. She would have loved to linger, but he didn't give her the chance.

"We'll find a different motel to stay in this time," Wyatt said as he rounded the Jeep to open the passenger door for her. "I think we should head out of Green Lake County, though."

"Good idea." She slid into the car, sternly reminding herself that Wyatt wasn't interested in her on a personal level.

He felt responsible for protecting her, nothing more.

Taking a deep breath to calm her racing heart, she glanced back at the sketch he'd set on the back seat. Seeing her father's features helped her focus on their mission.

She wasn't here to kiss Wyatt or cry in his arms. When had she turned into a crier anyway? This wasn't like her.

The most important thing was to find her dad. Steeling her spine, she lifted her chin and silently promised not to let Wyatt distract her.

Wyatt drove out of the sheriff's department parking lot and headed east. She glanced at him in surprise. "I thought you wanted to get out of the county?"

"I do, but rather than heading northwest, I'd rather find something closer. Appleton should have plenty of places to stay, and it's not somewhere the bad guys would expect to find us."

She nodded slowly. It was a good point, even though deep down she didn't like being so far away from the last place her father had been. "That works."

As they pulled onto the highway, Wyatt asked, "Are you hungry?"

Her earlier nausea had faded, leaving a gnawing in her stomach. Glancing at the dashboard clock, she was surprised to see it was six thirty in the evening. The events at the burned farmhouse along with the subsequent time spent at headquarters to provide their statements had taken longer than she'd realized. "I could eat, but we might want to wait until we're closer to the hotel. I feel like we should get out of Green Lake right away."

"Okay. We'll find another fast-food place and use the drive-through to pick something up." He sighed, then added, "Sorry, but it's probably safer in the long run than sitting down in a restaurant."

"Fine with me. It's not as if I haven't been living off fast food for the past few weeks."

He winced. "Now I feel guilty for not taking you somewhere decent."

"Don't be silly. It's fine." Going to a nice restaurant with him would feel way too much like a date. Something she hadn't done in a very long time.

Hard to maintain a relationship when you were constantly on the move.

"We need to formulate a game plan," he said after a few minutes. "The only thing we've learned so far was that Johnny Raffa's men keep coming after us."

"Do you know anything else about Raffa that might help us?" She felt as if they were grasping at straws. "Other than he seems to have limitless men willing to do his dirty work."

He was quiet for a moment. "Even if I had access to the FBI database, I wouldn't be able to trust the information listed there. Hawthorne could have very well doctored the data."

She understood his rationale. "Okay."

"You mentioned going to the burned farmhouse because it was the first place you and your dad used as a safe house."

"Yes, that's correct."

"Where did you plan to go after that?" Wyatt asked.

"The original house we lived in when we were Amish." She turned to face him. "I mentioned it earlier, but forgot once Liam and Garrett arrived. My dad might be waiting for us there."

He frowned. "You really think so?"

"Yes. That old house is the same place the Marcheses used when they kidnapped my sister, Rachel." Her heart thumped with excitement. Going there was the right decision. She just knew it. "I have a good feeling about this."

"Hold on, I don't think heading there now, in the dark, is smart," he cautioned. "I like your idea, though. It's a good plan to check that location next."

"We need to go now," she insisted. "Tomorrow might be too late. My dad might be there, waiting for us. He left that message for me, which tells me he's moved on and might be expecting me." She grabbed his arm. "Please, Wyatt."

He reluctantly nodded. "Okay. Where is this place, exactly?"

Good question. She tried to envision the abandoned house in her mind. "It's in the northwest corner of Green Lake County. Liam knows the address. He and Garrett showed up there shortly after I helped rescue Rachel."

Wyatt exited the interstate, then turned to get back on in the opposite direction. She was so glad he'd agreed to head to the abandoned house. She truly believed her father was there right now. He was just one step ahead of them, and she didn't want him to have to wait too long for them to show up.

She only wished she'd suggested it sooner. Well, she had, but then had gotten distracted.

This was why she needed to avoid getting too close to Wyatt. She sighed. At least they were on the right track now.

"Call Liam, and see if you can get the address." Wyatt headed back into Green Lake County. "We may need them to back us up, anyway."

She reluctantly dug out her cheap phone. Not that she didn't appreciate the possible need for back-p, but if her dad was there, they wouldn't need it.

The idea of getting her father to safety buoyed her spirits. She made the call, but Liam didn't answer.

"Liam, this is Abby. Call me when you have a minute." She disconnected. "He didn't answer, but I'm sure I can find the place without Liam's help."

He nodded, his gaze focused on the road. "I believe you."

She clasped her hands in her lap, silently praying they'd find her dad at the house where they'd lived together as a family before the Marchese men had found them.

A life she didn't really remember, other than a brief memory of picking flowers with Rachel that they'd presented to their mom.

Mammi. The Pennsylvania Dutch word for mom flashed in her mind. In May, when she'd found Rachel for the first time since they'd been separated, her sister's Amish dress had reminded her of the time they'd picked wildflowers.

She wished her memories of her mother were clearer, but living with her dad as a four-year-old through adulthood had replaced those early years.

Rachel had confided that their mother had passed away last year. Abby was sad about that, but the news had made her even more determined to make sure her dad was safe now.

"We're going to stay on this road all the

way into the Amish community," she instructed. "Be careful, there may be some horse and buggies out on the roads."

"I noticed a few earlier." Wyatt glanced at her. "Could you go back to living a simple life? One without electricity or other modern conveniences?"

"No." She honestly couldn't imagine how Rachel managed each day. "Although I like Green Lake better than Chicago. With my sister living there, I've been thinking it may be a good place to put down roots. I'm pretty sure my dad will agree."

"I've spent eight years in Chicago and grew up in Minneapolis, attending college there, too, before heading to Quantico for training. I've always been partial to big cities, but there is something nice about being in a place where you know your neighbors," he agreed.

"I've never been in one place long enough to become chummy with the neighbors." She and her dad had moved every few years, which had been detrimental to her grades. By her junior year she'd gotten her GED rather than trying to acclimate to a new high school environment. "No college, either."

"I'm sure that must have been difficult for you." Wyatt reached over to take her hand. "Once this is over you can attend college."

"Not likely." College tuition was expensive, and she barely had a few hundred bucks to her name. "But it will be nice not to be on the run, constantly looking over my shoulder."

"If you could attend college, what would you study? What career would you choose?"

She stared down at their hands for a moment before shrugging. "I can't say that I've thought too much about having a career. My goal has been to survive."

"You must have had dreams, Abby," he persisted.

"Maybe a cop." She flushed and shrugged. "I know that probably sounds stupid, especially since I've never trusted law enforcement. But watching the Marchese men trying to ruin Rachel's life, my life and my dad's makes me want to put more criminals behind bars."

"I think you'd be an amazing cop," Wyatt said. "You have excellent instincts."

She was glad for the darkness hiding her face, as her cheeks warmed. "Thanks, but I don't think there's a law enforcement agency in the entire country that would consider my application. Not with my lack of formal schooling and zero references. But that's okay," she hastily added. The last thing she wanted was sympathy. "I don't mind hard work. And frankly, having a regular job where I didn't have to hoard cash, in case I needed to run, would be amazing. I enjoy cooking, I'm sure I can find restaurant work in the Green Lake area."

"Don't underestimate yourself," Wyatt said. "You have more life skills than most of the cadets entering the police academy."

He was sweet to say that, but she was a realist.

Being a cop, or even working a regular nine-to-five job wasn't in her immediate future.

She'd happily settle for a simple life where she and her dad were no longer in danger.

It bothered Wyatt to realize just how much Abby had been through over the years. Even more sobering to hear that her goal was to have a regular job where she didn't need to feel the need to save up cash for a quick getaway.

Once this was over, he'd see if there wasn't a way that he could help her obtain a job in law enforcement. If that was truly what she wanted.

Yet he doubted he'd have a job himself with the FBI when this was over, so his offering a reference might backfire. It was more likely that they'd both be looking for new jobs when the danger was over.

Maybe they could stay together, too. He shot her a quick glance, remembering those moments he'd held her in his arms. He'd been unable to resist kissing her, and he'd struggled to keep it casual and comforting.

Abby had been on the edge of a breakdown. He'd known he couldn't take advantage of her momentary weakness.

Calm logic was one thing, but it had taken every ounce of willpower to keep from sweeping her close and deepening their kiss.

He drew in a steadying breath, preparing himself for their foray to the house where Abby and her parents had lived when they were Amish. He would have rather approached in the daytime but hadn't been able to argue her point about her father potentially seeking shelter there.

Having Peter Miller safe and staying with them would help in numerous ways. For one, he was hopeful Abby's dad would have some information that would help him find the proof he needed to bring down his boss, Ethan Hawthorne.

But even better, he could leave Peter and Abby together while he went out to find the bad guys. He was sure Liam would assist on finding them a place to stay.

It would be easier for him to continue the investigation if he didn't have to worry about two innocent people getting hurt in the cross-fire. Even if that meant he wouldn't see Abby for a while.

A flash of pain struck deep at the thought of leaving her behind, but he'd always known their partnership was temporary. Best to re-member that being on the run from bad guys did not exactly provide a foundation to build a future.

Besides, even if he didn't stay with the FBI, he didn't want to risk getting his heart broken a second time. Not after the way Emma had stomped all over it.

"Turn right to head north at the next in-tersection," Abby said, pulling him from his thoughts.

"Got it." He made the turn, surprised to see several houses dotting the landscape. The windows weren't ablaze with light, but sev-eral had a low, flickering glow from a lantern. "We must be in the Amish community now."

"Yes," she agreed. As they passed another sprawling property sporting a house and a barn, she gestured toward them. "That's where Rachel and Jacob live."

"Your sister?" He was surprised. "How do you know that?"

"Liam mentioned Rachel and Jacob were married recently." She shrugged. "Back in May I also followed Tony Marchese there. He planned to use Rachel as bait to draw out my dad. I was able to sneak up behind him as he was holding Rachel at gunpoint, hitting him in the head."

"Impressive." He grinned. "See? I was right about you having great instincts."

"It was more about being in the right place at the right time," she said modestly. "I was grateful to be of help. And it wasn't all for Rachel, either. Even if she escaped, I knew Tony wouldn't rest until he'd found me and my dad. Taking him out of the picture was the only option."

"Yet here we are, still in danger." He sighed. "All because of a dirty FBI agent."

She nodded, then put a hand on his arm. "Slow down, I don't want to miss the turn in the dark."

He eased down on the brake, scanning the area up ahead. The highway roads here were curvy, and despite the acres of farmland they'd passed, there were also several wooded spots, too.

"See that gravel road? That will take us to the house."

"I see it, but I'm not going to drive right up, Abby." He rolled past the gravel driveway. "We'll find a place to leave the Jeep and go in on foot."

"You're right." She relaxed against the seat. "I'm just anxious to check it out. There's a small opening between some trees about a half mile from here that would be a great spot to hide the Jeep."

As she made the comment, he saw the opening between two groups of trees. He slowed down, went past it, then stopped and put the Jeep in Reverse. The vehicle had a rear camera, which was helpful as he backed into the opening so they could make a quick getaway if needed.

When they were well covered by the fall foliage, he shut down the car. "I assume you know how to get to the house through the woods?"

"I do." She flashed a smile. "We'll go slow, though, so that we don't scare him off if he's hiding inside."

"Fine with me." He slid out from behind the wheel, taking a moment to quietly shut the car door. Abby did the same. He held back, waiting for her to take the lead.

She moved silently, obviously accustomed to approaching places without being seen or heard. He was impressed with her ability to avoid the dry leaves and branches scattered over the ground.

The wooded area wasn't large, so it didn't take them long to reach the clearing. She paused there, staying behind a large oak tree as she surveyed the abandoned structure.

He stayed beside her, searching for a sign that Peter Miller was waiting inside. Or maybe he was waiting somewhere outside. Thinking back to the first cabin where he'd found Abby, he was sure her dad had melted into the trees to avoid being seen.

Wyatt knew it was highly likely her dad would have done the same thing here. He leaned down to speak in her ear. "Should we split up, see if your dad is hiding in the woods nearby?"

"No." Her voice was so soft he barely heard her. "I think I should go toward the house. Once Dad sees me, I'm sure he'll come find me."

He scowled in the darkness. "Better we stay together."

"I need you to trust me on this."

Had she forgotten what had happened the last time they'd split up at the burned farmhouse? The gunman had almost struck her down with a bullet. A ball of fear lodged in his throat. He snagged her arm. "Please stick with me."

"I won't be long." She shook off his hand and darted forward. Thankfully, the lack of streetlights within the Amish community helped hide her in the darkness, especially as she wore dark clothing. For a moment he lost track of her, then saw the barest shadow of her crouching near the corner of the house.

He pulled his weapon and prepared to follow. The excuse of her father's lack of trust wasn't enough to hold him back.

When Abby moved along the side of the structure toward the back corner, he left the cover of the trees. Running silently, he held his breath until he reached the house, too.

But there was no sign of Abby. Assuming she'd gone around the corner, he quickly followed the same path she'd taken.

Peering around the corner, he expected to see her, but there was no one there. He frowned, then edged around the corner, belatedly realizing there was an open window on this side.

Remembering how Abby had escaped through a bedroom window when he'd first confronted her, he had no doubt she'd gone inside this way. He inched forward, intending to do the same, when he saw movement in the trees.

Abby's father? He instinctively dropped to the ground, just as a crack of gunfire rang out.

He sprang up, and threw his leg over the windowsill. Ducking beneath it, he fell into the room as a second crack of gunfire rang out.

"Wyatt?" Abby called softly.

"Stay down." He rolled to his feet, then ran from the room. Another gunshot came from what sounded like the front of the house.

If they didn't find a way to escape, they'd be trapped!

THIRTEEN

More gunfire? Abby crouched on the floor near the kitchen cabinets, hoping they would help prevent bullets from getting all the way through.

How was it these men knew where to look for them?

One possible answer was that they were familiar with the house because the Marchese men had used it as a place to keep Rachel after they'd kidnapped her.

And she had unwittingly walked into their trap. A wave of guilt hit hard. Her insistence on coming here had put Wyatt in danger.

"Abby, we need to get out of here." Wyatt darted forward and crouched next to her. "There are at least two men out there."

"I know, I've already called 911 but I'm not sure how long it will take for them to respond." She tried to think of the best way to escape, since staying put seemed like a bad idea. "If there was a way to create a diversion, we can try to make a run for it out back toward the trees."

"I'll create the diversion so you can escape." Holding his weapon in hand, he inched toward the closest window. "Ready?"

"No, I'm not leaving you." She reached out to grab his arm. "We're in this together, Wyatt, remember?"

Even in the dark she could see his frustration. "There's no time. The deputies will hopefully arrive soon to help me. It's more important that you get out of here."

"Not without you." She began searching the warped and dilapidated kitchen cabinets for something useful. But there was nothing.

Two more gunshots echoed through the night. She glanced over at Wyatt, who was still stationed near the window. He peeked over the edge, took aim, fired, then ducked back down.

If she had a gun, she could fire out the opposite side of the house. Fearing that gunman was making his way toward them, she quickly scooted to the window facing that way.

"Stay down!" Wyatt said in a harsh whisper.

Ignoring him, she sneaked a look over the edge of the window, praying the gunman wasn't racing toward them. She knew there was a very real possibility these two men could take them out before the deputies arrived.

Please, Lord, keep us safe in Your care!

There was no sign of the gunman outside, so she lowered her head and glanced toward the narrow hallway leading to the bedrooms. She'd heard Wyatt take a shot from the bedroom earlier but worried the gunman might come in that way.

Just as she was about to crawl toward the hallway, she saw movement. "The hallway!"

Wyatt turned and fired twice at the opening. She heard a grunt and sounds of movement. Before she could say anything more, Wyatt peered through the window and fired another shot.

How much ammunition did he have? What if he ran out? She swallowed hard, telling herself there was no point in worrying about something she couldn't change.

Flat on the floor, she stared toward the hallway, knowing the gunman would make a second attempt to kill them

If he was able. It seemed wrong to pray that Wyatt had hit him someplace that would make his ability to continue firing at them impossible.

After Wyatt had taken another shot through the kitchen window, there was a long silence. In her mind she imagined the outside gunman making his way toward the ramshackle house, intending to silence them once and for all.

Then she heard police sirens. Faint at first, then growing steadily stronger. She met Wyatt's gaze without saying anything.

She knew their thoughts were identical, each hoping the sound of the police would scare the shooters still hanging around outside away.

Wyatt stayed where he was, his gaze and weapon focused on the hallway. Her phone rang, and she quickly answered Liam's call. "Liam? There are two gunmen here, maybe more."

"I have four deputies on the way, ETA less than a minute and I'm right behind them," he told her.

"Okay, thanks." She lowered the phone. "One minute."

True to his word, Liam arrived. She saw flashing lights through the open windows. Still, she and Wyatt didn't move, waiting for the deputies to clear the area.

"Abby? Wyatt?" She recognized Garrett's voice. "Are you okay?"

"Yes," she called back. "But there is a gun-man in the house, possibly injured."

"Coming in." The sound of footsteps was as reassuring as the sirens. Garrett came into the kitchen, his gaze sweeping over the two of them, before turning toward the hallway.

A second deputy was hot on his heels, taking up a flanking position behind Garrett.

"Police! Keep your hands up where we can see them!" Garrett's demand was answered with nothing but silence. He gave the second deputy a nod, then carefully made his way down the hall, his back pressed against the wall.

She held her breath and prayed for their safety.

"One perp down," Garrett called out a minute later. "He's alive."

"Thank You, Lord Jesus," Wyatt whispered.

"Amen," she echoed.

"Wyatt, you and Abby stay where you are until my deputies have cleared the property," Garrett warned.

"We will," she answered for them both. Then she crawled toward Wyatt, giving in to the need to stay close at his side. "I'm so sorry, Wyatt. This is my fault."

"You didn't shoot at us." He holstered his

weapon, then wrapped his arm around her shoulders, bringing her close. "But I have to admit that was way too close."

"It is my fault! I never should have insisted on coming here at night." She desperately wished she hadn't pushed the issue.

"I'm sure the gunmen would still have been here, anyway, waiting for us," Wyatt said soothingly. "And maybe they would have hit us in the daylight."

He was being too sweet and kind in letting her off the hook. Yet if Wyatt had suffered an injury, or worse, been killed here tonight, she'd never have forgiven herself.

"Don't stress," Wyatt murmured as if reading her mind. "Our future is in God's hands."

"I know." She pressed a grateful kiss to his cheek. "I still feel bad at how this turned out, though."

Before Wyatt could respond, Garrett called out from the bedroom.

"Liam tells me the outside perimeter has been cleared and secured," he said. "I need you both to come in here."

Wyatt scrambled to his feet, drawing her up beside him. Together they joined Garrett and his fellow deputy.

A gunman was lying on the floor, his eyes closed as he held his arm. The gun he'd used had been kicked into the corner of the room, and she assumed Wyatt had hit his dominant arm, making it difficult for him to return fire.

"Who are you?" Garrett asked, as she and Wyatt knelt beside the injured man. "Who sent you?"

The man averted his gaze and didn't reply for a long moment.

"You need to talk," Wyatt said firmly. "Do you think Raffa is going to support you in jail? Not likely. He'll be angry that you let yourself get caught and arrested. You failed to carry out his orders. He'll cut you loose faster than you can blink."

The injured gunman grimaced, then finally said, "The orders didn't come from Raffa directly, but from his top enforcer, Bubba Graves."

Wyatt sucked in a loud breath, drawing Garrett's attention. "I take it you know Bubba Graves?"

Wyatt nodded. "I've heard of him, but have never seen him. To my knowledge he hasn't done any time, so his prints are probably not in the system. His nickname is the Grave Digger because he allegedly puts down the competition and buries the bodies."

"Great," Garrett muttered.

"Okay, so Bubba sent you. What did he

order you to do? Kill Abby and her father?"
Wyatt pressed.

"To kill the fed, the woman and the old
man," he corrected.

The fed? Abby stared at Wyatt, who looked
grim.

And she knew his boss would not stop until
all three of them were dead.

The gunman's comment packed a punch,
even though Wyatt had known he was a target. He had no doubt Hawthorne was working
with Raffa and the Grave Digger to silence
him, permanently.

No way was Wyatt going to let him get
away with this.

He focused his attention back on the gunman. "Who was shooting at us from the front
of the house?" He pinned the gunman with
an intense look. "What's his name? Where
can we find him?"

"Joe Avery…" The gunman closed his eyes,
then whispered, "I don't know where he went."

"You must have an idea." Wyatt wanted
to shake the man, but managed to keep his
hands to himself. "Who is he? There's no reason for you to be loyal to him. He left you
here, didn't he? Come on, give us an idea
where to find him!"

Eyes closed, the gunman didn't answer.

"Wake up. Can you hear me? At least tell me your name!" He couldn't hide his desperation.

"I'm sorry, Wyatt, but we need to get him to the hospital," Garrett said. "I promise we'll continue to question him once he's been treated."

Wyatt swallowed a wave of frustration, forcing himself to take a step back. The good news was that he hadn't killed this guy. Maybe Garrett and Liam would be able to get more information out of him.

Hopefully, not before it was too late. After this latest attack, he felt certain they were running out of time. Especially after the way these gunmen had stayed one step ahead of them from the very beginning.

"Wyatt? Abby?" Liam's voice caused him to turn toward the doorway. "You're both okay?"

"Yeah." He raked his hand through his hair.

"I'm sorry I missed your call, Abby," Liam said, his face mirroring guilt. "I wasn't on call. Shauna and I try not to use our cell phones at dinner unless I am on call."

"It's okay. This is my fault." Abby sighed. "I'm not used to working with law enforcement. I should have waited for you to respond before heading here."

"No, I should have answered your call." Liam stepped out of the doorway to allow two EMTs to enter. They went straight to the injured man without delay.

For several minutes no one spoke, giving the EMTs the time and space they needed to care for their patient. Only when they had the man strapped to the gurney and wheeled away did Wyatt turn toward Liam.

"He mentioned getting orders from Bubba Graves, aka the Grave Digger, top enforcer for Johnny Raffa. It might be helpful if you and your deputies could dig into him. See if anything has surfaced about him."

"We will," Liam assured him. "Do you and Abby need a ride?"

"No, we still have the Jeep."

"It's parked well off the road, deep in the brush," Abby added. "We wanted to walk in, rather than drive directly to the house."

"It's a good thing you did," Garrett said. "What I'd like to know is how the gunmen knew to stake this place out in the first place."

"If you dig deep enough in the property records, Peter Miller's name is listed as an owner twenty-three years ago," Liam said. "That's why we came here searching for Rachel after she was kidnapped."

"I didn't realize that," Abby admitted. "I

mean, I knew we lived here but I didn't know that my dad's name was listed as the owner."

"I'm sure my boss dug into every piece of intel I had on Peter Miller," Wyatt said grimly. "Before I even realized he was dirty."

Abby rested her hand on his arm. "He's the bad guy in this, not you. I'm the one who insisted on coming tonight."

"Let's take a moment to be grateful we all survived without being hurt." Liam offered a wry smile. "It's pointless to ruminate over what could have been done differently."

"You're right," Wyatt agreed, feeling ashamed. "We are truly blessed to have arrested one of the hit men. We know that the Grave Digger is giving the orders. If we can find him, we may find a link to my boss."

"We'll do our best," Liam promised. "Why don't I escort you to the Jeep?"

"Sure." Glancing around, he knew there wasn't much he could do here. "Liam, do you need to take this weapon as evidence, too? If so I'll need a replacement."

Liam grimaced and nodded. "Yeah, I do. You can take my weapon. I'll get a replacement at headquarters. I'll give you an extra clip, too."

"Thanks." He hesitated, then added, "I can

pay you for the gun and the clip since it's clear this isn't over."

Liam sighed. "Yeah, you're right about that. Here." He pulled a Glock and clip from his belt.

He squashed a flash of guilt, accepting the weapon and ammunition. "Thanks." He pulled out some cash, but Liam shook his head.

"No need." Liam turned and led the way down the hall and out the front door of the house. "After everything you two have been through, it's the least I can do."

More guilt washed over him. Liam was treating him as an equal within the law enforcement community, even though he was technically on leave from the Bureau.

The walk back to the Jeep didn't take long. Liam led the way, with Garrett following close behind. Wyatt appreciated their support considering the deputies had already cleared the area.

Just to be on the safe side, he borrowed Liam's flashlight and once again crawled under the Jeep to make sure there were no tracking devices. When he was satisfied the vehicle was clean, he rose to his feet and handed the flashlight back. "Thanks."

"Keep it," Liam advised. "I have more at headquarters."

He nodded, and tucked it beneath his arm. "I'm sorry we had to drag you out tonight."

"I don't like knowing these mafia hit men are lurking around my county," Liam said grimly. "Be careful."

"Will do." He opened Abby's door, then went around to get in behind the wheel. As he pulled forward from their hiding spot, he glanced at the rearview mirror, noticing both men were still standing there, talking.

"Guess we need to find that hotel," Abby said, breaking the silence.

He nodded, deciding to take a different route back to Appleton. Based on how the events had unfolded, he felt certain the gunmen had been waiting for them, rather than following them to the house, but he'd rather err on the side of caution than risk putting Abby in more danger.

They'd been shot at more than enough over the past forty-eight hours.

"Wyatt, I need a gun."

Abby's statement caught him off guard. "No, you don't. I'll protect you."

"I do need one. I could have taken the back side of the house, providing cover to keep the gunman from getting inside," she insisted.

"I almost grabbed the one the gunman used that was lying off in the corner of the room, but I knew Liam and Garrett needed it for evidence."

He blew out a breath. "It's better you didn't take that one, Abby. They absolutely do need it for evidence. Especially as I wounded the guy."

"I know. That's exactly why I didn't take it." She twisted her fingers in her lap. "But I don't like feeling helpless. I would rather be armed when we go into another dangerous situation."

She wouldn't need to be armed if she stayed back, but he knew offering that as a solution would not fly. Abby would insist on going with him, no matter what. "Okay, I'll talk to Liam in the morning. Don't get your hopes up," he warned. "He's been giving me weapons to use because I'm a fed. You're not. And to legally buy a gun you need to have a background check done."

"It's fine if Liam does a background check on me. I've never been arrested."

"That's great, but it doesn't mean he'll do that and agree to sell you a gun." If the situation were reversed, he wouldn't be so quick to arm a civilian.

"Liam's a good man. I'm sure he won't mind."

He wasn't convinced Liam would do any such thing, but he let it go for now. Their priority was to find a safe place to stay for what was left of the night.

If such a place existed.

It wasn't easy to keep the defeatist attitude from getting to him. Knowing Bubba Graves was giving the orders didn't really help them very much.

A wave of exhaustion hit hard, the aftermath of the adrenaline crash. He did his best to shove it aside, staying focused on the highway ahead of them, while keeping a keen eye on the rearview mirror.

"Are you sure you don't blame me for making us go to the house tonight?" Abby asked.

"I'm positive. Like I said, they may have been able to target us sooner in the daylight." He hesitated, then added, "I didn't see any evidence of your father being there, did you?"

"No, and that's why I'm kicking myself for going at night." She sighed and threaded her fingers through her hair. "I didn't see any messages written on the walls or what was left of the kitchen counter, but we didn't get to examine the place more closely, either. What if we missed something important?"

"The place will be crawling with cops for the next hour. If there's something in there, they'll find it." He glanced at her curiously. "A note is fine, but it would be easier if your dad called you."

"I know, I keep thinking there must be a good reason he hasn't." She frowned. "I assume he lost the phone and hasn't had time to replace it yet. Or that he hasn't been in one spot long enough to recharge the battery."

He couldn't argue; she knew her dad better than he did. They fell silent as he continued driving north of Green Lake County, crossing toward the city of Appleton.

Lights dotted the horizon, indicating they were getting close. He didn't stop at the first place he saw advertised, but did pull off the highway at the next one.

He used his badge to convince the clerk to give him connecting rooms for cash. A few minutes later, he unlocked both doors, handing Abby a key.

She knew by now to open the connecting room door. He opened his side, then dropped into the closest chair.

"Hey, you look worn out." Her gaze was full of concern as she joined him, pulling a second chair close. "I haven't thanked you for saving my life."

"No need." His attempt to smile failed miserably. "I hate knowing how much danger you're in. That we're all in."

"Don't, Wyatt. This isn't our fault." She held his gaze for a long moment, then surprised him with a kiss.

All rational thought fled from his mind, as he hauled her close and kissed her. Deep down, he knew that any attempt to keep Abby at arm's length was useless.

It was too little, too late. He'd already fallen for every inch of her stubborn resilience.

She had his heart, whether she wanted it or not.

FOURTEEN

Kissing Wyatt was amazing, but she was the one who'd instigated this embrace.

Not him. He was sweet, strong and protective. He wouldn't want to hurt her. Which meant she needed to gather the willpower to step back. Fighting regret, she pulled away.

"I—uh…" She fumbled for words to express how she was feeling. It was tempting to blurt out how much she'd come to care for him, but she didn't want to ruin the camaraderie they'd shared. "We should get some sleep."

"Yes, we should." His low, gravelly voice sent shivers of awareness down her spine.

Swallowing hard, she took another step toward the connecting door. "Good night, Wyatt."

"Good night, Abby."

She forced herself to walk away. After getting rid of the layer of dust and dirt she'd accumulated in the abandoned house, she connected her two disposable phones, the one she used with her dad, and the one Wyatt had obtained from Liam, then crawled into the bed.

Despite her physical exhaustion, the gunman's words echoed through her mind.

The orders came from Raffa's top enforcer, Bubba Graves... kill the fed, the woman and the old man.

It was discomforting to know some strange man had given his team orders to kill her along with both Wyatt and her father.

All because some greedy fed wanted to keep his dirty little secret.

She did her best to push those thoughts aside and calm her mind. Praying helped, and she wondered if Rachel found a similar peace with prayer.

At times like this, it was easier to understand why her Amish twin had chosen the simple life. Granted, Rachel had been in danger, but from outsiders, not those within their peaceful Amish community. It would be nice to settle down in Green Lake once the danger was over.

If the danger was ever over.

Taking several deep breaths, she imagined pushing her worries up toward God, letting them go like balloons floating away in the wind.

She must have fallen asleep, because the

next thing she knew, a chirping sound dragged her away. She lunged for the phone, bringing it up to her ear. "Dad? Is that you?"

There was a long silence, but she thought she heard heavy breathing on the other end of the line. Then the call abruptly ended.

Rolling to her feet, she clutched the phone tightly. Was the call from her father? Had he been about to speak, but then couldn't?

Her dad was the only one who had this number. No one else. She shoved her feet into her shoes, then crossed the threshold into Wyatt's room.

"What's going on?" Wyatt was sitting on the edge of his bed, blinking the sleep from his eyes. "I heard a phone."

"I think my dad tried to call me." She couldn't seem to loosen her grip on the device. "I only heard breathing and then silence. But I know he's out there and in trouble."

Wyatt nodded. "I understand your concern, but we still don't know where to find him. He could be anywhere in Green Lake, or even in the entire state of Wisconsin. Even down in Chicago."

Logically, she knew Wyatt had a point. But she couldn't let what she instinctively knew was a cry for help go.

"We need to head back to the cabin in the woods, the first place you found me."

He arched a brow. "Why?"

"I don't know!" She dragged a hand through her tangled hair. "I think my dad was staying there, at least for a while. But he stayed hidden when he noticed you were following me. We know he's not in the burned farmhouse, or the house we just left. I think our best move is to head back to the cabin, the place where he had been safe. Just like he wrote on that wall."

He sighed. "It's one o'clock in the morning. We need to wait until daylight."

"We can't wait." She couldn't shake the impending sense of doom. "We have to go now, Wyatt. Not in six hours. Please, I need to see for myself if he's there." And not injured, or worse.

She could see the indecision in his eyes, but then he nodded. "Okay, but we'll call the sheriff's deputies on the way. I'd like them nearby in case we run into trouble."

"I don't want them to scare him off." She held his green gaze. "Let's wait until we know for sure my dad is actually there, then call them."

She could tell Wyatt didn't like it, but he took a moment to put on his shoes, then stood. "Okay, let's go."

The worst part about going tonight was that she wasn't armed. Granted, she didn't know for sure if Liam would have allowed her to carry a gun, but she didn't like feeling vulnerable.

Hopefully, she wouldn't need one. If they determined her dad was there and unharmed, she'd convince him to come with them. If her dad was in trouble, they'd get the sheriff's deputies involved.

Satisfied they had a decent plan, she followed Wyatt outside to the Jeep. Always on guard, he scanned the area carefully before opening the passenger door for her.

"Thanks." She slid into the seat, as he came around to do the same. "I'm glad you chose this hotel. We're actually closer to the cabin."

A hint of a smile curved on his face. "It wasn't intentional." Then he frowned. "If I remember correctly, the cabin isn't located within Green Lake County. The sheriff's deputies won't have jurisdiction there."

She winced and nodded. "I'd forgotten that. But knowing Liam and Garrett, I'm sure they'll still respond if we need to call for help."

"Probably." He kept his gaze on the road. "Just keep in mind, if we have to call 911 the

call will likely go to the county with jurisdiction."

"I don't care. Any cop is welcome." Ironic
to realize her mistrust of cops in general had
disappeared over the past few days. Wyatt,
Liam, Garrett and the other deputies who'd
all responded to their calls had proven most
cops were decent men, committed to fighting crime.

The real bad guys here were Johnny
Raffa and Ethan Hawthorne. Without those
two, even Bubba Graves and his henchmen
wouldn't have orders to kill them.

Her nerves wouldn't settle as Wyatt drove
through the night. She glanced at him, knowing he was only doing this because she'd
asked him to.

Anyone else would have refused to run off
in the middle of the night on what very well
may be a fool's errand.

"I appreciate your support, Wyatt." She
lightly touched his arm. "I know you're doing
this against your better judgment."

He smiled wryly and shrugged. "I've come
to trust your instincts, Abby. I'm hoping everything is fine, and your father's phone ran
out of battery."

She didn't believe that for a minute, and
sensed he didn't, either. "Except for the fact

he made contact for the first time in the middle of the night." The breathing on the other end of the line reminded her of the brief contact she'd had with her father a month ago. That time he'd said her name, then had abruptly ended the call.

Tonight, she'd gotten the impression he'd been running and then dropped the phone.

Running from Bubba Graves's gunmen? She didn't want to believe it, but even Wyatt had mentioned that his boss had every bit of intel he'd gathered on her father.

If Raffa or Bubba had been tracking their bad guys or been in league with them, they may have assumed her dad would return to that cabin.

There was no traffic on the highway as Wyatt took the highway back to the cabin. She noticed he didn't pull off in the spot where she'd left her sedan that had been towed after the wheels had been taken out by the shooter. She frowned as he kept driving. "Where are you going?"

"Looking for signs of a vehicle." He shot her a quick glance. "I figure if the gunmen are here, they probably have a ride stashed someplace close by."

It was a good thought, but it would not be

easy to find a hiding spot in the darkness. "If they were smart they'd have it well hidden."

"True. But they're not always smart." He waved a hand. "Besides, we need to find a similar type of hiding spot for the Jeep."

"Okay." She reined in her impatience. Better to go into the woods prepared for anything, than unexpectedly stumble across a couple of bad guys intent on harming them.

Wyatt drove for what seemed like forever. He made a large loop around the wooded area, as much as he could, considering the highways were located far apart.

When he made a second pass, he slowed the Jeep. "See that area up ahead?"

"Yes." There was a narrow opening between several large trees located about fifty yards off the road.

"Hang on." Wyatt slowed, but then went off road, the Jeep rocking back and forth as he navigated down a culvert and back up over the debris. Branches scraped along the underside of the Jeep. Instead of driving straight in, he made a tight turn so he could back into the space, the same way he'd done at the abandoned house that had once belonged to her family.

A family torn apart by the Marcheses eighteen years ago, and again now by Johnny Raffa.

Wyatt shut down the engine, then turned to face her. "I'd like you to stay inside the Jeep for a moment. I need to make sure we didn't leave tire tracks announcing our location."

She wanted to argue, but realized she would only slow him down. "Okay."

Wyatt slipped out of the vehicle, softly shutting the door behind him. She could just barely see him as he moved in the darkness, dragging a large tree branch back and forth over the indentions made by their tires.

A few minutes later, he returned. "It would be better if you waited here for me to clear the cabin."

"No, I'm coming with you." She needed to see her father for herself.

"Fine." He sounded resigned as she quickly slid out of the Jeep to join him. "Stay behind me," he added in a whisper. "I'm armed. You're not."

She nodded, understanding his logic as she closely followed in his footsteps. She was blessed with a good memory related to geography and knew they were approaching the log cabin from the opposite direction from where she'd come in through the woods a few days ago.

After ten minutes of silent walking, Wyatt stopped. He crouched behind a tree, drawing her down beside him. He put his mouth near her ear. "The cabin is roughly fifty yards ahead."

She took a moment to get her bearings, then nodded. "I agree."

"I don't smell smoke. Do you?"

She slowly shook her head. The scent of pine trees and damp leaves was in the air, but nothing like that first night when she could smell the wood-burning stove well before she reached the cabin. "No. But that doesn't mean my dad isn't hiding inside."

The thought of the cabin being a dead end filled her with dread. Even if the bad guys had captured her dad, wouldn't they start a fire to stay warm? The temperature was only forty degrees. Not freezing, but not warm enough to simply sit around doing nothing.

She squelched a sense of helplessness. They'd come this far; it wouldn't take too long to clear the cabin.

Yet Wyatt didn't move for several long moments, seemingly listening intently. She did the same, knowing that sounds of humans moving through the woods would indicate they were not alone.

The night was eerily quiet. Almost too quiet.

And the overwhelming sense of doom grew more acute with every passing second.

For the tenth time in as many minutes, Wyatt wished Abby had stayed in the car. He didn't want her to be anywhere near the cabin.

Especially since his nerves were jangling in warning.

"I need you to wait here so I can get a little closer." He spoke as quietly as possible. When he sensed a refusal coming, he added, "Please, Abby. Do this for me. I'm armed and you're not."

After a long moment, she whispered, "Okay, but if you're not back in ten minutes I'm calling 911 and coming after you."

"I promise I'll be back in the allotted time frame. And don't forget, I can call you if I find your dad inside." If the area wasn't safe, he would use every ounce of his expertise to avoid being caught by Raffa's goons. "I just want to get a little closer to see better."

She nodded and moved into a more comfortable position behind the tree. He gave her a quick kiss of gratitude, then rose and silently moved forward.

Despite the ten-minute alarm clock ticking

off the seconds in his mind, he didn't rush. Silence was more important than speed. And he wasn't too far away. Abby could probably still see him.

After he'd made it twenty yards closer to the cabin, he paused and listened again.

If the bad guys had Peter Miller inside, he felt certain there would be voices indicating their presence. On the other hand, if Peter was alone, he likely wouldn't be talking to himself.

He didn't hear a thing. Either Peter was alone, or the cabin was empty. His gut wouldn't settle down, though, and if he were honest, he'd admit he did not believe the place was empty.

As such, he continued moving silently, determined to avoid being drawn into a trap. If he were the Grave Digger, he'd remain quiet until the last possible moment.

Raking his gaze along the side of the cabin, he changed his trajectory so that he could move forward while keeping a wary eye on the back door.

When he was only ten yards from the cabin, he paused again to listen. Still no voices, but then he heard a creaking board.

A footstep?

He hesitated, unsure if he should risk moving forward. He didn't hear anyone talking, so maybe Peter Miller was hiding out inside alone.

Rising to his feet, he was about to step forward when the back door opened, revealing two men wearing black.

Both carrying guns.

He froze, hoping, praying they hadn't seen him. Without making any sudden movements, he slowly edged closer to the nearest tree.

By his internal clock, he still had two minutes left before Abby would call 911 and follow him to the woods. Carefully reaching into his pocket, he wrapped his fingers around the phone.

The two gunmen spread out and began walking toward the woods, their actions clearly threatening as they held their weapons ready. If they came too much closer, they'd surround his hiding spot.

Keeping the phone in his pocket, he took his gaze off the threat looming before him to send Abby a quick text.

Two gunmen. Call for help.

Dropping the phone back in his pocket, he eyed the two men, hoping he could take one of them by surprise.

He didn't think they could have heard him approach. Not from inside the cabin.

Unless they had someone else keeping watch somewhere nearby?

His chest tightened at the possibility. No! Not Abby!

Please, Lord Jesus, keep Abby safe in Your care!

Wyatt understood what he needed to do. He had to eliminate the threat. The gunman closest to him took another step closer. Wyatt lifted his weapon. "FBI! Drop the gun!" When the gunman spun toward the sound of his voice, he didn't hesitate to fire. The gunman groaned and dropped to the ground, clutching his chest, but Wyatt was already searching for the second shooter.

There! He caught a glimpse of movement through the trees. The guy turned, his gun pointed at Wyatt, so he quickly aimed and fired. At first he thought he'd missed, but the gunman had slumped against the closest tree before sliding to the ground.

Before he could take another step, he heard a voice shouting from inside the house. "Drop your weapon, Wyatt, or I'll shoot the old man in the head."

The voice sounded familiar, but he didn't think it was Hawthorne. It sounded nasal, as if the man inside the cabin suffered from allergies.

Regardless whom the voice belonged to, Wyatt couldn't risk anything happening to Peter Miller. The assailant knew his name. "Okay, there's no need to shoot. I'm coming out, see?" He held both his arms over his head, as he took the three steps necessary to get to the clearing. When he was in sight of the cabin, he made a big show of tossing the gun in his hand far off toward the downed men. "I'm not armed."

"Move slowly forward. If you make any sudden moves or do something stupidly brave, I'll shoot you and the old man, then look for the woman later."

"Okay, I won't do anything stupid." The fact that the guy had said he'd look for the woman later gave him hope that his men didn't have her. That Abby would get out of this alive.

Even if he and Peter died today, he would take heart in knowing Abby was safe. He didn't mind sacrificing his life for hers.

The only regret he'd have was that he hadn't told her how much he cared for her. Loved her. The realization punched him in the gut. He'd only been with her a few days, but the attraction was there from the start, and as they'd traveled this dangerous path together, his admiration, respect, and, yes, love, had grown over time.

"I'm near the door," he called, unsure if the gunman holding Peter Miller hostage wanted him to come all the way inside. He stood, his arms over his head, and mentally braced for the impact of a bullet.

"Oh, please, come in and join us," was the sarcastic response. The nasal voice was even more familiar now, but it wasn't until he opened the door and stepped inside that he understood just how wrong he'd been.

All this time he'd believed Hawthorne to be the mole inside the Bureau, but the man standing with his gun pressed against Peter Miller's temple was his partner.

Allan Trudeau.

FIFTEEN

Seeing the two gunmen coming outside the cabin had sent a chill down Abby's spine. She was just about to call 911 when Wyatt shot twice, taking both men out. Her relief was short-lived, because a voice from inside the cabin told Wyatt to drop his weapon and keep his hands up, or the old man would die.

Her father.

She quickly made the 911 call, explaining in a hushed whisper about a man with a gun holding her father hostage. She gave the woman the location to the best of her knowledge, using the highway marker she'd memorized years ago.

"Please stay on the line," the woman said.

"I can't. There could be others. Please send help as fast as possible." Without waiting for a response, she disconnected from the line, then made one more call, this time to the Green Lake Sheriff's department. She'd called 911 first thinking they might be closer, but she hoped deputies from both counties responded to the threat.

Liam and Garrett were likely home sleeping, so she quickly updated the dispatcher, letting him know that Liam and Garrett would know the location of the cabin. Once that call had been made, she shut her phone off and jammed it in her pocket.

That was the easy part. Now came the hard part. No way was she going to sit here and do nothing while Wyatt faced the danger alone.

There was no doubt in her mind he would sacrifice himself for her.

For her father, too. But the way things looked, both Wyatt and her dad were in grave danger. She silently acknowledged that if she went to the cabin unarmed, all three of them would die. She'd heard the gunman threaten to come after the woman, meaning her.

Yet what choice did she have? None.

Then she remembered the two gunmen Wyatt had taken out. Her pulse kicked up. Could she find one of their weapons? Yes! She took a deep breath and began making her way silently through the woods, moving faster than normal because she knew time was of the essence.

How long before the man inside the cabin simply shot Wyatt and her dad?

Minutes, not hours. And that was only if Wyatt was able to stall for time.

Yet despite her need to hurry, she was careful to keep an eye out for more shooters. There seemed to be a never-ending supply of them, and for all she knew there were more nearby.

Please, Lord, bless us by keeping all of us safe in Your care!

Thankfully, it didn't take her too long to reach the spot where she'd seen the two gunmen go down. Creeping on her hands and knees, she searched the brush for his gun. It wasn't easy as the darkness made it difficult to see much of anything. Still, she gently padded the ground as she moved toward a man's body.

Just as she was losing hope, her fingers snagged on something heavy. She cautiously picked it up and lightly brushed off the damp leaves sticking to the metal.

Still on her hands and knees, she backed away from the body so that she was deeper in the woods. From there, she rose to a crouch and quickly made her way to the side of the cabin where the two bedrooms were located.

She'd gone through the window to escape

Wyatt what seemed like eons ago. Now her goal was to crawl back inside the same way.

Finally she was positioned across from the bedroom window. She could hear deep voices coming from inside, which reassured her the window was still open.

She lightly ran across the clearing, then bent down near the window. The two male voices were louder now, and she could hear Wyatt trying to reason with the man he addressed as Trudeau, who must be the one holding her father.

Not Hawthorne? His identity didn't matter to her right now, so she tucked the gun in her waistband, then carefully climbed through the window.

"There's still time to turn yourself in." Wyatt's tone was calm. "Why risk killing a fed?"

"I'm killing a dirty fed," the nasal voice corrected. She assumed he was Trudeau. "That's how this is going to look by the time I'm finished with you and the others. Hawthorne trusts me, and already believes you're dirty."

"I know several local cops, including a sheriff who know the truth. They are not going to believe I did this and they will hunt you down," Wyatt said firmly. "I told them all about the dirty fed inside the Bureau. It won't take them long to finger you if they haven't done so already. You already lied about your hernia surgery. That was obviously a sham. Give it up, Allan. Don't make things worse for yourself."

"Yeah, I have to admit I expected more from the Grave Digger," Trudeau said in a disgusted tone. "But trust me, I'm good. I will make sure the evidence against you is so overwhelming that your local yokels will have no choice but to agree with my findings."

Abby froze inside the bedroom for a long moment, then let her breath out in a soundless sigh. The voices had helped muffle any noise she'd made getting in through the window.

She pulled the gun from her waistband and crept carefully to the doorway.

"Call the woman and tell her to come here," Trudeau said. "Or I'll shoot the old man."

Abby's breath caught in her throat. They were running out of time!

"You're going to shoot him whether I call Abby or not," Wyatt said. "Meanwhile Abby is already on her way to safety."

"Call her!" Trudeau's voice rose sharply.

"I'm telling you, she's already someplace safe." Wyatt spread his hands. "Peter, do you want me to call Abby?"

"No." Her father's hoarse reply hit her like a ton of bricks.

She moved down the hall toward the main living space where Wyatt stood a little off to the side of the room to her right, near the wood-burning stove, which was not lit. As she stepped closer, she could see her dad was shivering in the cold, tied to a chair, but his gaze was resolute, as if he'd accepted his impending death.

Considering how a short man with dirty-blond hair had his gun pressed tightly against her dad's temple, she couldn't blame him. The way Trudeau stood to the side with his gun against her dad would make it difficult for her to get a clear shot at him.

She swallowed hard, moving another inch closer while trying to catch her dad's eyes. He needed to be ready to pull away at the right time.

Her dad's gaze seemed focused on Wyatt. Staring hard, she subtly tried to draw his attention, without giving herself away to Trudeau.

"Face it, Trudeau, it's over," Wyatt said. "Abby has escaped and you'll be found guilty of murder."

"Call her, or I'll shoot you and use your phone to call her myself." As if to demonstrate, he moved his weapon away from her father, aiming at Wyatt.

The moment Trudeau's weapon moved away from her dad she fired the weapon in her hand, striking Trudeau in the abdomen. He doubled over, his face registering shock, but didn't go down.

At the exact same time, her dad leaned sideways, tipping his chair over so that he was lying on the ground, his hands still tied behind his back. And Wyatt threw himself at Trudeau, who somehow managed to still hang on to his gun.

The two men struggled for the weapon and another gunshot rang out, making her jump.

Wyatt? She rushed forward, trying to get a clear shot at Trudeau. But then Wyatt yanked the gun from Trudeau's grip and rolled off him. The dirty FBI agent fell lax onto the floor.

"Are you hurt?" She was torn between checking Wyatt for a gunshot wound and helping her father out of the chair.

"No, the shot went high." He scrambled to his feet, holding the weapon on Trudeau, who was still groaning in pain from his belly wound. "Check your dad."

She was already kneeling beside her father, trying to untie the knots holding him to the chair. Wyatt joined her, using his knife to cut through the binds while he kept an eye on Trudeau, who now appeared completely out of commission.

"Dad? Are you hurt?" She searched his gaze, running her hands down his arms and legs.

"Nothing serious." Her dad grimaced and struggled to his feet. "You were supposed to be safe," he accused.

"Tell me about it," Wyatt muttered. "Although I had a feeling she'd do something like this."

"I wasn't leaving either of you, but I did call for help." She couldn't help looking at Trudeau. Yes, he was a bad guy, and would have killed her dad, Wyatt and her, too, without blinking an eye. Yet she felt guilty for shooting him.

Easier to aim and pull the trigger at a paper bull's-eye, rather than at a living, breathing person. Her hands began to shake. She tried to control the trembling.

"Thanks for saving our lives," Wyatt said, putting his arm around her shoulders. "I was worried there was another gunman in the woods who had found you. Each time Trudeau ordered me to call you, I felt certain you'd gotten away."

"There's one guy, Bubba, who is still out there somewhere," her father said. "Although if you ask me, he was probably smart enough to skip town."

Another gunman? Even as the thought flitted through her mind, Wyatt was yanking her and her father down just as several rounds of gunfire hit the cabin.

Wyatt pushed himself in front of Abby and Peter, trying to ascertain which direction the bullets were coming from.

He'd hoped Abby hadn't been found, but he should have anticipated there would be another gunman on the loose.

"Trudeau is shot," Wyatt shouted. "It's over! Throw down your weapon!"

He didn't really think Bubba Graves would do as he'd asked, but he was hoping to pinpoint the guy's location.

Bubba didn't answer, but there was more gunfire, this time not directed at the cabin. "This is the Marquette County sheriff's department. We have you surrounded. Drop your weapon and put your hands on your head where we can see them!"

The deputies had arrived!

"Green Lake County sheriff's department

is here, too," another voice called out. "There is no escape. Surrender your weapon, now!"

Wyatt stayed right where he was, with Peter and Abby sandwiched between him and the kitchen cabinets. He wasn't going anywhere until the deputies had cleared the area of assailants.

Thankfully, Bubba must have realized that if he didn't comply, he would likely die.

"Got him," someone shouted.

"Let's clear the area," another said.

"Three innocents in the cabin, one dirty cop down with a belly wound," Wyatt shouted.

"Wyatt, is that you?" Liam's familiar voice asked.

"Yes, with Peter and Abby Miller, too."

"Stay put, we're coming in. The rest of you, make sure the woods around this cabin have been cleared, understand?"

A chorus of "Roger that," echoed in response.

Two minutes later, Liam and Garrett entered the cabin. Garrett knelt beside Trudeau, while Liam came over to where he was sitting.

"So this is Hawthorne?" Garrett asked.

"No, actually it's my former partner, Allan Trudeau." Wyatt still couldn't believe he'd pegged the leak as his boss, rather than his partner. The fake surgery had been a good diversion. Something he hadn't anticipated.

"Help me," Trudeau whispered.

"Once we clear the area, we'll get you to the ambulance waiting on the highway," Garrett said. "If you want to tell us who to look for, that job would go faster."

Trudeau groaned and muttered something Wyatt couldn't hear. "What did he say?"

"Sorry, I'm not sure. It was gibberish to me." Garrett shrugged. "No name, that's for sure. I doubt there's anyone else out there."

Wyatt hoped he was right. He rose, then turned to help Abby to her feet. Peter looked weak, but stood without assistance. "Peter, how long have you been here?"

"In the cabin? For a couple of days." The older man flushed. "I should have come forward when I saw you and Abby here that first night, but I didn't trust you, Agent Kane. I still believed you ratted me out."

Wyatt nodded. "How have you been getting around?"

"An old motorcycle that I've hidden a mile from here." Peter cracked a smile. "I was almost caught by a gunman. That was when I broke off the call with you, Abby. Then I ran out of battery. It was only recently I was able to recharge it. While hiking here to the cabin, I called Abby but then saw another shooter." He grimaced. "I dropped the phone and kept running."

"Oh, Dad," Abby whispered. "That's scary."

Peter grimaced. "I'm so sorry you were put in a position to rescue me."

"Hey, she rescued both of us," Wyatt said wryly. "You obviously taught her well."

Peter shook his head. "I did my best, but I'm obviously not that good. I shouldn't have let Trudeau get the drop on me. I knew better than to stay in one place for too long."

"I'm glad we came to find you," Abby whispered.

"Me, too," Wyatt agreed.

"The deputies have given the all clear," Liam said. "Technically this cabin isn't my jurisdiction, but the Marquette County deputies were okay with us taking over from here. Especially when I mentioned how several other crimes were committed by these same bad actors in Green Lake County."

Wyatt was secretly relieved to be working with cops he knew and respected. "Thank you."

Two deputies carried Trudeau out of the cabin to meet up with the EMTs making their way in from the road. His partner had lost consciousness, and Wyatt hoped he survived the shooting. He didn't want Abby burdened with the death of the man she'd shot, and he needed to know how his partner had gotten access into his files on Peter Miller.

Was it as simple as watching him enter his password and copying it? Or had he somehow hacked into his laptop? Trudeau was good with computers, and he often worked the financial side of the organized crime business.

It made him wonder how long his partner had been working for the mafia as an insider. Rubbing a hand over the back of his neck, he was troubled at how much money Trudeau could have hidden on behalf of the Marcheses and more recently for Johnny Raffa.

Everything his partner had done was suspect now and would require an in-depth investigation.

One thing that still bothered him was how quickly his boss, Ethan Hawthorne, had agreed with Trudeau that Wyatt was the guilty party. As far as he'd known, Trudeau hadn't been aware of his meeting with Peter Miller that day that gunfire nearly killed him. Had Hawthorne mentioned it? Or had Trudeau hacked into his computer to find the information, himself?

"Wyatt? Are you okay?" Abby's voice drew him back to the important issue at hand.

"I'm fine." He longed to pull her into his arms, but held back under the watchful eye of her father. There would be time to express his feelings, later.

"I'd like the three of you to provide brief statements, for now," Liam said. "We can get a more detailed description later."

Wyatt didn't argue. Liam drew him to the side, leaving Abby to talk to Garrett while another deputy took Peter Miller off to the opposite corner.

The retelling of the events didn't take that long. Liam recorded the conversation with his phone, rather than taking notes. As an FBI agent, Wyatt knew it was important to get key information right away, when memories were fresh.

"Do you and Abby need a ride back to Green Lake?" Liam asked when they'd finished.

"We have our Jeep hidden in the brush about a mile north of here." He glanced over to where Abby was still talking to Garrett. "We have Peter now, too. I'm sure Abby will convince him to come with us to the hotel."

"If you could all come down to headquarters again sometime late tomorrow morning, that would be great." Liam pocketed his phone.

"That's fine. I'll have to call my boss in the morning, too." Wyatt knew he should do that right away, but he was too exhausted and knew Hawthorne would want him to recap every detail. "I'd like to know when Allan Trudeau is awake and talking. My boss is going to want to interview him, ASAP."

"He was taken to Appleton but will likely be transferred via helicopter to either Milwaukee or Madison. Those cities have the only two level-one trauma centers in the state."

"If you could let me know which one, I'd appreciate it."

"I will." Liam glanced around the cabin. "You and Abby did great work today."

"Thanks, but we're alive because of Abby." He wanted Liam to know how much she deserved all the credit. "She would make a great cop."

"Yeah?" Liam glanced thoughtfully to where she was finishing her interview. "Is she interested in joining the force?"

"I think so." He hoped he wasn't poking his nose where it didn't belong. "She doesn't have a college degree, though, so that may hold her back. Maybe you or Garrett could talk to her more about that tomorrow."

"Sounds good." Liam sighed, then added, "Maybe you should wait until early afternoon to stop by. We're going to be here for a while yet."

He chuckled. "Why don't you call me when you're ready? That way you can take your time."

"I will." Liam crossed over to meet with Garrett and the deputy who'd questioned Peter.

"Are you ready to get out of here?" Wyatt glanced at Abby and her father. "We might be able to get back to the hotel in time to get some sleep."

"And food," Peter said with a crooked smile. "I haven't eaten much."

"We'll find something along the way," Wyatt promised. "It's a long hike back to the Jeep, though."

"We'll be fine, right, Dad?" Abby put her arm around her father's waist. "You can lean on me."

"I can walk," Peter said firmly. "Lead the way, Agent Kane."

"Wyatt," he corrected. "I promise I'm on your side and Abby's."

Peter nodded but didn't say anything more. Wyatt sensed he was saving his energy for the upcoming hike to the car.

There was no point in moving quietly, but he still took a path with less foliage so they could move faster. He glanced back over his shoulder several times, to make sure Abby and her father hadn't fallen too far behind.

It took almost twenty minutes to reach the Jeep. He paused, waiting for Abby and Peter to catch up, when he heard a rustling sound.

He turned, in time to see a man emerge from the brush. For the second time that night, his heart just about stopped in his chest.

A paunchy, bald guy stood holding a gun pointed directly at him, and it took him a moment to recognize Rex Jericho, the Chicago Chief of Police.

Another dirty cop!

SIXTEEN

The moment Wyatt stopped abruptly Abby knew something was wrong. Her dad had been moving slowly, so they were roughly twenty feet behind him. She quickly pulled her father deeper into the brush.

"Shh," she whispered in her dad's ear. "Trouble."

He nodded and crouched behind a tree. She stood near him, straining to listen.

"What brings you here, Chief Jericho? You're a little outside your jurisdiction, aren't you? Chicago is a hundred and ninety miles from here."

"Shut up," a strange male voice snapped. "Where are the Millers? They were right behind you."

"Peter Miller was injured by my former partner, Allan Trudeau. The cabin is crawling with cops. You're not going to get away with this."

"I told you to shut up!" The blatant panic in the police chief's tone concerned her. Abby had been about to call Liam, but there wasn't time. Unfortunately, she also didn't have a weapon, as all the weapons had been taken as evidence.

She felt along the ground until she found a large rock. The angle wasn't good, so she put a hand on her dad's shoulder, silently warning him to stay down, as she moved sideways to find a better position.

"Where are the Millers?" Jericho shouted. "I want them here right now! I need to get rid of all three of you once and for all!"

"I don't know, I told you the old man is hurt. They could be a half mile back for all I know." Wyatt spoke calmly, the same way he had when facing off with his corrupt partner.

She knew he was vying for time. It wasn't easy to pinpoint the chief's location in the dark, but after two more steps she saw the barest hint of moonlight illuminating the back of his bald head.

Without hesitation, she brought her arm back and threw the rock at him with as much force as she could muster.

Thwack! It struck him on the back of his head. The man grunted and stumbled forward. Wyatt sprang at him, yanking the gun from his hands and then wrenching his arm up behind his back.

Abby ran forward. "Are you okay?"

"I'm great, thanks to you." Wyatt smiled, then turned his attention to his prisoner. "How nice of you to bring your own handcuffs." Wyatt pulled them from the cop's belt and quickly shackled his wrists together. Then he took Jericho's gun and placed it in his holster and patted the guy's legs.

"What are you doing?" Abby asked.

"Making sure he doesn't have a backup weapon. Like this one." Wyatt pulled a small revolver from an ankle holster.

"Glad you thought of that." She stared down at the man for a moment. Abby was shocked she'd hit her target. At best, she'd hoped to distract him long enough for Wyatt to disarm him.

The man groaned again but didn't move.

"Nice arm, Abby. You should be playing on a woman's softball team." Wyatt glanced up at her. "Where's your dad?"

"Here." Peter came up behind her. She reached out to put a hand on his arm. "I had no idea the Chicago police chief was involved in this."

"Yeah, I had suspected a few dirty cops, but not him." Wyatt rolled the chief over on his back. The man's eyes were closed, but Abby was relieved to note he was still breathing. "Jericho was brought in as chief ten years ago. When I joined the FBI, we noticed an uptick of organized crime, and wondered what was going on." He scowled at the man on the ground. "Now we know."

"Jericho must have been working with your partner." Abby was still trying to wrap her mind around the entire situation.

"Yeah, and Jericho must have been the one in a position of power," Wyatt agreed thoughtfully. "It seems to me that Jericho stayed hidden, forcing Trudeau do the dirty work. And only when he'd failed, decided to take matters into his own hands."

"Why didn't he just run?" Abby asked. "If he'd disappeared, he probably would have gotten away with it."

Just then, the chief's radio squawked. Abby couldn't believe when she heard Liam's voice come through the speaker asking for an update on the crime scene techs' arrival. That was when she understood. "Jericho was listening in the whole time?"

Wyatt nodded. "Appears so. He knew Trudeau wasn't dead and must have been worried the truth would come out."

Abby blew out a sigh. "And that's how he

avoided being caught by the deputies that cleared the area."

"Exactly." Wyatt reached down to take the radio. He used it to respond. "Liam? We have the Chicago chief of police, Rex Jericho, here in handcuffs. He pulled a gun on me and threatened to kill all three of us."

There was a pause, before Liam asked, "Where are you?"

"I don't have the exact coordinates, but we're roughly a mile northeast of the cabin," Wyatt said. "I'll turn on the Jeep headlights so you can find us."

"Roger that. Be there soon," Liam said.

"Unlock the Jeep, Wyatt," she said. "My dad should sit down for a bit."

"You got it." Wyatt dug out the key fob and unlocked the car. He stared down at the chief. "I'm surprised he didn't have backup with him."

Abby glanced around worriedly. "Let's hope he doesn't."

"Sorry, I didn't mean to scare you. If there had been anyone here, they'd have shown themselves by now," Wyatt hastened to reassure her. "It just struck me that he must have been handling things at a higher level to ensure the Marchese and Raffa families were able to get away with their crimes."

"You think there could be more dirty cops involved?" Abby asked.

"I think there must be." Wyatt sighed, then opened the driver's-side door and slid behind the wheel. He powered the Jeep's engine, the headlights shining brightly in the night. "Liam will find us easily enough now," he joked.

"Yes, he will." She shut the door, huddling in the back seat beside her father. Their nightmare was over. Granted, there would be a cleanup among the ranks as the chief was arrested and prosecuted, along with Allan Trudeau from the FBI, but that wouldn't involve her or her father.

"Hang on, I think that might be Liam and a few of his deputies." Wyatt shot a reassuring glance at her, then slid out of the Jeep. "Stay inside where it's warm, okay?"

"Thanks." Her chest tightened as she realized this might be her last few hours with Wyatt. Sometime tomorrow, maybe after they spoke with Liam, he'd have to head back to Chicago to meet with his boss about Trudeau and the police chief. She had to assume Wyatt would be busy uncovering the extent of corruption that had infiltrated both law enforcement agencies.

Leaving her and her father to resume and rebuild their lives.

A wave of sadness hit hard. She didn't want things to end this way. Yet the idea of going to Chicago did not appeal to her in the least.

No, she wanted to stay in Green Lake, close to her sister, Rachel. It felt nice to know she could settle in one spot rather than constantly being on the move.

She wasn't worried about finding a job at a restaurant, although she didn't want to work as a server or even as a cook forever.

"What's wrong, Abbs?" Her father used her nickname as he reached for her hand. "You look sad."

"Oh, I'm not." She forced a smile. "I'm glad we found you, and that the dirty FBI agent and police of chief won't cause any more trouble."

"I feel bad for thinking Wyatt Kane set me up," her dad acknowledged. "I'm glad he was helping to keep you safe."

"He was amazing." She spoke softly, even though Wyatt was outside talking with Liam. "I wouldn't be here if not for him."

"Seems like you did your part in saving Wyatt, and me, too," her dad pointed out. "I'm proud of you, Abbs."

"Thanks." She told herself it was enough to know she and her dad were safe and together at last.

Still, she watched Wyatt, her heart yearning for something she could never have.

"This night keeps getting more and more interesting," Liam said dryly. "First a dirty agent, then a dirty chief of police. Are you sure there aren't any politicians involved?"

"No, I'm not," Wyatt said honestly. "But you can be certain my boss and those higher in the Bureau will be looking under every rock we can find to make sure no one else is involved."

"You did great work here, tonight," Liam said in a more serious tone. "If you ever decide to make a career change, we'd be happy to have you as part of our team. Abby, too. I plan to talk to her more tomorrow, see what her thoughts are about the future."

"I'm glad you're considering Abby. She gets the credit for taking Jericho out with a rock." Wyatt stared thoughtfully at Liam. "I hadn't thought about working as a local law enforcement officer."

"Hey, I get it." Liam raised a hand. "You're way overqualified to be a deputy. I just happen to have two men who are retiring at the end of the year and figured I'd mention it. No pressure, I will certainly understand if you'd rather stay where you are."

"I'm honored," he admitted, his thoughts whirling. He'd mistakenly blamed his boss for being the leak, but discovering his own partner had tried to kill him was just as bad. He'd always planned to have a career within the Bureau the way his father had, but it was difficult to imagine going back and picking up where he'd left off. "Will you give me some time to think about it?"

Liam looked surprised. "Of course."

"Thanks." He glanced at the Jeep, unable to see Abby and her father because of the headlights shining so brightly, but he was sure they would not be interested in heading back to Chicago, either. Abby had mentioned her intent to stick around Green Lake to be closer to her sister. Peter would want to do the same. "I'll see you later, okay?"

"I'll call you," Liam said. He and Garrett had hauled Chief Jericho to his feet. The man swayed a bit, but was awake, his gaze darting from Liam and Garrett back to Wyatt.

"You don't have anything on me," the chief protested.

"We have you threatening to shoot a federal agent and two civilians," Wyatt corrected. He wasn't in the mood for dealing with the dirty cop. "Get him out of here, Liam. I'm too tired for this."

"Let's go." Liam tugged on the chief's arm. "I'm sure you know your rights, but I'll tell you them anyway." As Liam recited the Miranda warning, Wyatt turned and climbed back into the Jeep. He let out a sigh of relief, then glanced over his shoulder at Abby and Peter.

"Ready to get out of here?"

"Yes, please," Abby said wearily.

"Me, too," Peter agreed.

"Let's do it." He put the Jeep in gear and pulled out of the hiding spot, navigating the uneven terrain to reach the road.

The trip back to the hotel didn't take too long. His passengers in the back were silent, and he was glad to see Peter was sleeping.

Once they were close to Appleton, he searched for a fast-food restaurant. Despite it being five in the morning, he was pleasantly surprised to find a place with lights on and an Open sign in the window.

"I'll order breakfast sandwiches and coffee for each of us, okay?" Wyatt asked softly.

"Yes, that would be great," Abby whispered back.

He purchased the meals, then drove straight to the hotel.

Peter lifted his head, sniffing the air. "I smell something great."

"Nothing fancy," Wyatt warned. "But it should take the edge off your hunger." He parked in front of the hotel and pushed out of the driver's side, carefully balancing the three coffees and bag of food.

"Thank you, Wyatt." Peter's tone was sincere as he took the coffee cup tray from him. "I owe you more than I can ever repay."

"Hey, this isn't your fault," Wyatt protested. He pulled out the key and unlocked the door. "Abby proved to be a great partner, and she would not rest until we'd found you."

"We were a great team," Abby agreed. She turned on the lights as he set down the bag of food. The room was cramped with the three of them, but they made it work.

Wyatt wanted nothing more than to talk to Abby alone, but of course, this wasn't the time or place. He unpacked the sandwiches as Peter set the coffee cups around the table.

"Wyatt? I'd like to say grace." Abby reached for her dad's hand, then took his, too. "Dear Lord Jesus, we thank You for protecting us and keeping us safe. We are humbly grateful to be here, eating this food You have provided. Bless us, Lord. Amen."

"Amen," Wyatt and Peter echoed. Glancing at Peter, he could see the man's eyes were suspiciously moist.

"That was beautiful, Abby," Peter murmured. "The entire time I was being held at gunpoint, I knew I was wrong to give up my faith."

"Wyatt helped bring me back to God," Abby said. Her gaze shifted from her father to his. "I know you would have sacrificed your life for me, Wyatt."

It was a statement, not a question, but he nodded. "Yes, of course. I couldn't believe it when you shot Trudeau. I was hoping you were far away from the cabin."

"So was I," Peter said dryly.

"I wasn't going to leave either of you." Abby smiled at her father, then added, "I knew Wyatt would do everything possible to save you, Dad. He is by far the most honorable man I've ever met."

"I wanted to save both of you," he corrected, even though his heart soared at her words. "I'm glad I was able to be there for you, Abby. And to help find you, Peter."

Peter's gaze shifted from him to Abby in a way that made Wyatt realize his feelings were probably clear to the older man. But Abby's father didn't say anything more, digging into his sandwich with gusto.

For a long moment they simply enjoyed the food, then Abby broke the silence. "What was that Liam said about a job? Yes, I was eavesdropping, but couldn't hear much."

He took a sip of his coffee, then set it down. "I told him he should consider hiring you as a deputy. I know you'll have to take the entrance exam, and go through the academy, but I'll help you study if that is something you're interested in. Honestly, Abby, I think you'd make a great cop."

"Me?" Her eyes widened. "That's not possible, I only have a GED."

"Anything is possible. You proved that over these past few days," he said. "And trust me, you're smarter than you're giving yourself credit for."

She still looked perplexed. "I thought Liam offered you a job."

He shifted in his seat, then nodded. "He did, yes. Apparently, he has two deputies who are retiring at the end of the year."

She eyed him over the rim of her cup. "But you're an FBI agent. I'm sure you're headed back to Chicago, right?"

"Wrong." In that second, he made up his mind. "I don't want to stay in the Bureau. I'm going to take Liam up on his offer. But my future depends on you, Abby." He glanced at her dad, then added, "I know the timing isn't great, but one thing this experience has taught me is that life is short. I care for you, Abby. Deeply. More than just care. I want to explore a relationship with you. I don't want to be far away from you, and I don't think either of you want to live in Chicago."

"I'll go wherever Abby wants, but not until I get a chance to visit my daughter, Rachel," Peter spoke up. "If she wants to see me, that is. I've been banished and shunned by the Amish, so she may not want to."

"She does, Dad," Abby quickly interjected. "Although I don't know all the Amish rules, I know Rachel wants to know you're okay. Even if it's only a brief meeting."

"That's good to hear." Peter smiled, ate the last bite of his sandwich, then added, "Sounds like you two need some time alone." He wiped his mouth with a napkin, rose and took his cup of coffee in the other room.

Wyatt wasn't going to waste a second of the privacy Peter had wisely given him. "I love you, Abby. I know you may not feel the same way as I do—we haven't known each other for long, but I hope you'll give me a chance to show you how much I care. I will go wherever you want, just as long as we're together."

She eyed him for a long moment. "I love you, too, Wyatt. I'm not sure how it happened so quickly, and I never imagined you felt the same way. Are you sure about this? I have nothing to offer you, except my heart."

"I would gladly take your heart, and your love, and your everything." His heart soared at her words. He stood and drew her to her feet. "I don't need anything but you, Abby. Only you."

She went up on her tiptoes to kiss him, and he wrapped his arms around her, holding her close. Things were happening fast, yet despite the short time frame, he knew Abby better than he'd known Emma.

Abby was twice the woman Emma was. She had risked her life for him. And for her father.

The way he would have sacrificed himself for the two of them, as well.

When she broke off their kiss, it took a moment for his head to clear. "I love you so much, Abby. And if you don't want to be a cop, that's fine. I just wanted you to know you had options. Choices." He searched her blue eyes, hoping he hadn't pushed too hard. "You're so strong I know you can do anything you set your mind to."

She smiled. "I may have been called stubborn a time or two," she teased. Then her expression turned serious. "Your faith in me is humbling, Wyatt."

"I have faith in us, and in God," he corrected. "And even you have to admit we made a great team."

"A cop." She chuckled and shook her head. "Funny how I once avoided law enforcement of all types. Now I'm seriously considering joining the police force."

"I'll support whatever you decide, Abby." He didn't want her to think she had to go that route. "You can work in a restaurant, or nowhere at all. I only want you to be happy."

"You make me happy," she said with a smile. "I'm sorry I threw that log at you the first time we met."

He couldn't hold back a bark of laughter. "Don't apologize. You were smart enough to catch me off guard."

She laughed softly. "Yeah, well, I've learned to be resourceful through the past few years."

"And that ability will be helpful no matter what career path you choose to take." He gathered her close. "All I care about is that you're happy."

"I am, too. I love you." She kissed him again, and Wyatt knew God had truly blessed him when He'd brought Abby into his life.

Thank You, Lord!

EPILOGUE

Three weeks later

Abby sat next to her sister, Rachel, who was holding on to their dad's hand. They were at a small restaurant where Rachel's café had once been located. Abby was surprised to discover that her sister had sold the property to a young couple, after discovering she and Jacob were expecting a baby.

"*Ach, daddi*, it's *sehr gut* to see you," Rachel said in a low voice.

"I'm so sorry that I had to leave you and your mother behind," Peter said somberly. "I only did it to keep you both safe."

"Rachel found the letter you sent shortly after you left," Abby said. She'd been touched at her father's sacrifice. "As much as I missed growing up with my sister—" she glanced at Rachel "—I'm glad I was there for you, Dad. And Rachel was there for our mom. We know you didn't want to go but felt you had no choice."

"That is true," her father admitted. "My father and brother were powerful men. I was so afraid they'd keep trying to find me…"

"And they did, *ain't so*?" Rachel said, her gaze full of sympathy. "Abby told me the frightening experience you've both suffered."

"All that matters is that we are here, now." Their dad smiled. "And we are going to stay in Green Lake, too."

"Really?" Rachel's expression brightened. "*Ach*, that would be wonderful." Then her expression turned sorrowful. "Although I may not be allowed to visit you, *Daddi*. The elders may not support my decision to have a relationship with you."

Jacob and Wyatt had been standing behind them, but now Jacob stepped forward. "Rachel, mayhap if we explain about the threat to your father and sister, Bishop Bachman and the other elders will soften their stance on Peter's banishment."

"You really think so?" Abby didn't know Jacob very well but could easily see that the tall, somewhat somber-looking Amish man would do whatever possible to make her twin happy.

"I do," Jacob said firmly. "It's very different leaving because of danger, rather than from choice, *ja*?"

"*Ach*, I pray you are right, Jacob," Rachel agreed. She turned back to their father. "*Denke* for coming to visit with me, *Daddi*. And you, too, Abby." Rachel's eyes grew bright with tears. "I care for you both, very much. And I'm so happy to hear you plan to stay in Green Lake."

"I care for you, too, Rachel." Abby had to swipe at the tears in her own eyes. "But Liam gets a lot of the credit for us being able to stay here. He's hired Wyatt as a deputy."

"I love it here," Wyatt said with a nod. "Being a part of Liam's team is an honor."

Abby smiled proudly at Wyatt. He'd given up his career with the bureau despite Hawthorne's apologizing for believing him dirty and begging him to stay. With the Marchese family members having been killed in prison, the Raffa crime family had become the FBI's organized crime division's top priority. The injured gunman had survived surgery and was now working with Hawthorne to give more information on the Raffa family's illegal business dealings. Interestingly, the former Chicago Chief of Police Rex Jericho had also decided to cooperate, in exchange for a lesser sentence. Between the two sources, the FBI had gotten the information they'd needed.

Trudeau had finally admitted to working with the Marchese crime family in exchange for a cut of their profits. Having grown up poor, Allan had been sucked in by the easy money. But when he'd learned about Peter Miller AKA Paulie Marchese providing information to Wyatt, he'd grown desperate. First he'd tried to kill Peter Miller at the designated meeting spot, then had done whatever he could to make Wyatt look guilty. Soon after, he'd worked with the Raffa family to kill Wyatt, Abby and Peter.

Wyatt had told her that Hawthorne himself had headed up the Raffa family raid, arresting the main players and putting an end to the danger once and for all.

For the first time in years, she felt safe. And she had Wyatt's sheer determination and grit to uncover the truth, to thank for that.

"And your sister is thinking of taking the police academy exam, too." Wyatt stepped up to rest his hands on her shoulders. Abby rested her hand on his, grateful for his never-ending support.

"*Ach*, that is wonderful news," Rachel agreed. "Liam and Garrett have been a blessing."

"Despite the elders' position against seeking help outside the community," Jacob added dryly. "Rachel, it's almost time to go. I'm sorry, but I must take care of the animals."

"Of course, we understand." Abby stood as did her father and Rachel. She gave her twin a big hug. "We will stay in touch, okay?"

"Sehr gut," Rachel whispered, returning her hug. "I love you, Abby."

"I love you, too." Abby stepped back so that her father could also embrace the daughter he'd been forced to leave all those years ago. Abby knew he had regrets, but there was no point in looking backward.

It was time to celebrate today and their future.

Wyatt cleared his throat loudly. "Ah, before you leave, I have an important question."

Abby looked at him in surprise, as did Rachel, Jacob and her father. Was he about to ask about the upcoming Thanksgiving holiday?

Did the Amish celebrate Thanksgiving? Abby realized she still had a lot to learn about the lifestyle her sister and Jacob embraced.

Wyatt stepped forward, then went down on one knee. He pulled out a small velvet box and opened it. "Abby, will you please marry me?"

Abby knew her family was grinning madly, but she only had eyes for Wyatt. In the past few weeks, they'd grown even closer, and she knew with every fiber of her being she loved this man, and he loved her. "Yes, Wyatt, I would be honored to be your wife."

"*Ach*, so beautiful, *ain't so*?" Rachel said.

"I'm happy for your sister," Jacob agreed.

"I'm happy for both of my girls finding men who love and will care for them," her dad added in a husky voice. "Praise the Lord."

Abby hugged Wyatt, kissed him, then went back to hug each of her family members, including Jacob. She eyed her brother-in-law. "You need to convince the elders to allow Rachel to attend our wedding."

"I will do my best," Jacob promised. "Hopefully, they will agree."

Abby believed him, especially when Rachel leaned against him, her hand resting on her abdomen. Wyatt slipped his arm around her waist and pressed a kiss to her temple. "I love you, Abby."

"I love you, too." She smiled. This was her family.

And she could feel God's love shining down and surrounding them.

* * * * *

Dear Reader,

I hope you've enjoyed returning to Green Lake and reading Abby and Wyatt's story. I've had so much fun writing these books and am currently plotting my next story, too. I don't have the idea fully fleshed out or written yet, but I do know my next story will feature sketch artist Jacy Urban. It's time for her to have her happily ever after, don't you agree?

I adore hearing from my readers! I can be found through my website at https://www.laurascottbooks.com, via Facebook at https://www.facebook.com/LauraScottBooks, Instagram at https://www.instagram.com/laurascottbooks/, and Twitter https://twitter.com/laurascottbooks. Also, take a moment to sign up for my monthly newsletter, to learn about my new book releases. (Like Jacy's story!) All subscribers receive a free novella not available for purchase on any platform.

Until next time,
Laura Scott